Georgetown Mysteries
and Legends

Georgetown Mysteries and Legends

by
Elizabeth Huntsinger Wolf

JOHN F. BLAIR
PUBLISHER   WINSTON-SALEM, NORTH CAROLINA

The paper in this book meets the guidelines
for permanence and durability
of the Committee on Production Guidelines for
Book Longevity
of the Council on Library Resources.

COVER PHOTOGRAPH
by Thomas Namey, Namey Design Studios (www.nameydesign.com);
taken at the historic Mansfield Plantation Bed & Breakfast
in Georgetown, S.C. (www.mansfieldplantation.com).

Library of Congress Cataloging-in-Publication Data

Huntsinger, Elizabeth Robertson, 1958–
Georgetown mysteries ad legends / by Elizabeth Huntsinger Wolf.
p.   cm.
ISBN 13: 978-0-89587-340-8 (alk. paper)
ISBN 10: 0-89587-340-0
1. Tales—Washington (D.C.) 2. Legends—Washington (D.C.) 3. Ghost
stories. 4. Georgetown (Washington, D.C.)—Folklore. I. Title.
GR110.W37.H86 2007
398.2509753—dc22   2006102124

For
Bob and Virgnia Lee

Contents

Acknowledgments

My husband, Bob, my daughter, Virginia Lee, and my parents, Alasdair and Virginia Robertson, have been a tremendous help and inspiration in the search for, telling of, and chronicling of mysteries, legends, and ghost stories.

I owe true debts of gratitude to the following:

Doc Baldwin
William Baldwin
Frank Beatty
Raejean Beatty
Becky Berry
Lee Brockington
Betty Brown
Geordie Buxton
Jo Camlin
Captain Ronnie Campbell
Ann Carlson
James Carolina
Charleston County Library South Carolina Room staff

Captain Dickie Crayton
Captain Sammy Crayton
Sam Crayton III
Bill Doar
Inge Ebert
Pearlene Flowers
Kelly Burch Fuller
Georgetown County Library family (I work there!)
Georgetown Times staff
Brian Henry
Sassy Henry
Jamie Houtz
Ann Ipock
Kaminski House Museum staff
Lori Lewis
Isabel Mayer
Barry McCall
Molly Mercer
Bill Oberst
Robbie O'Donnell
Alma Owens
Gene Roberson
Gwenevere Tucker
Jesse Tullos
United States Coast Guard National Vessel Documentation Center staff
Billy Weaver

Prologue

Mysteries and legends—historic Georgetown County, South Carolina, abounds with them. It is natural that an old seaport area known for its ghosts would have its share of mysteries and legends, too.

Built on the peninsula where the Black, Pee Dee, Waccamaw, and Sampit rivers flow into Winyah Bay and then the Atlantic Ocean, Georgetown received International Port of Entry status from Great Britain in 1732. Since that time, Georgetown and the surrounding seacoast and countryside—from the colonial seaport to the pirate-era fishing village of Murrells Inlet, from the wind-swept sea islands to the fertile rivers and woodlands—have been blessed with a storied legacy.

The history of Georgetown is interwoven so intricately with legend that the two have become inseparable parts of one vivid and many-textured fabric. After all, most legends begin as oral history. Inexplicable events, unresolved through time, have remained mysteries and become legends.

Many of Georgetown's historic personalities were so passionately strong-willed in their loves and causes that their passage from this life into the hereafter left ethereal imprints.

Those imprints—which have lingered for decades or, in many cases, for centuries—are the ghostly hauntings chronicled in my first two books, *Ghosts of Georgetown* and *More Ghosts of Georgetown*.

While ghostly imprints from a long history of passionate living are abundant here, many of Georgetown's vibrant historic lives left mysteries and legends—but not ghosts.

Why?

We may never know.

Although *Mysteries and Legends of Georgetown* contains several ghost stories, most of the tales in this book detail uncanny, unexplained events that have left no hauntings. A couple of stories are neither unresolved mysteries nor ghostly hauntings. They are relics from Georgetown's historic past that are just downright bone-chillingly eerie—and needed to be set down on paper.

Georgetown County's special *je ne sais quoi* transcends explanation and makes it different from any other place on earth. There is a haunted, blessed, historic edge here that nurtures a sense of connection with the past.

Leaving behind the brilliant lights of Myrtle Beach and crossing the Georgetown County line into Murrells Inlet, one feels a distinct alteration in the atmosphere. In the words of Pawleys Island writer Ann Ipock, "it's as if a curtain drops somewhere around Murrells Inlet, and there's a change in the air."

Behind that curtain, one enters a landscape of barrier islands, coastal inlets, magnolias, ancient live oaks, and Spanish moss—the Low Country ambiance. This sometimes surreal landscape encompasses a mélange of colonial, Revolutionary War, antebellum, Civil War, late-Victorian, and twentieth- and twenty-first-century perspectives—a breathtaking setting for the lives played out here over the centuries. Many of those lives left us with ghostly hauntings. Others did not. Instead, they left a tantalizing legacy of mysteries and legends.

Many people have asked me—at storytelling events, at book signings, and in the kerosene lamplight of my Ghosts of Georgetown Lantern Tours—for more Georgetown tales. In answer to those requests, here is another collection—*Mysteries and Legends of Georgetown.*

" . . . magic casements, opening on the foam
Of perilous seas, in faery lands forlorn."

> John Keats, "Ode to a Nightingale,"
> reprised by Captain Daniel Gregg in
> *The Ghost and Mrs. Muir*

"The Owl and the Pussy-cat went to sea
In a beautiful pea green boat."

> Edward Lear,
> "The Owl and the Pussy-cat"

Storm Ball
October 13, 1893

During the darkest hours before dawn, miles out at sea and unbeknownst to any man, a fierce hurricane swirled its way northwest through the Atlantic. For days, the storm had been gathering strength as it traveled the open ocean.

With every mile, the storm drew closer to its predestined landfall—Magnolia Beach in Georgetown County, where those living on the edge of the ocean were blissfully unaware of their impending fate. No one knew of the hurricane's approach except one creature—a mermaid who hoped with all her being for a raging flood.

How did this mermaid know of the approaching hurricane?

Why, she had a storm ball! Landlocked high and dry in an old bathing house up near the sand dunes, she watched her water-bearing glass storm ball day and night, hoping the water would overflow. If the water inside her storm ball rose high enough to trickle out, this would point to a drop in air pressure, heralding a great storm. The mermaid fervently hoped for a tempest ferocious enough to send the ocean water surging through the bathing house, which would wash her out to sea where she belonged. If only she could get back into the sea, she would never again be curious about humans.

Weeks ago, one night at high tide, she had left the water and crept across the sand to the bathing house. Curious about the people who went inside to change clothes before frolicking at the edge of the ocean, she slipped through the door to look around for some of the peculiar items they brought with them. All she found was a partial loaf of bread. It smelled so good! She picked it up and took a bite. It was delicious. She took another bite before creeping back out to the surf and swimming away.

The next night, she crept back into the bathing house, drawn by the smell of fresh bread. As she bit into the end of a newly baked loaf, she heard the creak of the door, then *slam!* She was shut up in the bathing house.

For weeks now, she had been trapped well above the high-tide line with nothing to quench her thirst save precious drops of rain from a leak in the tin roof. Day and night, she listened to the crashing of the waves, the ebb and flow of the tides, and the incessant patter of rain on the roof. It had begun raining when she was first locked in and had been raining ever since, so no human had ventured down to the bathing house to change clothes for a swim in the sea. She had seen no one except the few who came to peer curiously at her.

Every day, the mermaid dejectedly watched the gray rays of sun filter through cracks in the clapboard walls. Hot and frustrated, the exquisite blue scales on her tail dulling from lack of seawater, she gazed forlornly at her storm ball, for it alone held foresight into her deliverance.

Rare and fragile, the storm ball was a delicately rounded clear-glass sphere with a slender glass spout rising up one side. A water barometer, it was invented by German playwright Johann Wolfgang von Goethe, who died in 1832. Goethe created the storm ball to operate on Torricelli's principle—the rule discovered in 1643 by Italian physicist and mathematician Evangelista Torricelli that air pressure is subject to change. A high-pressure weather system, such as arrived with fair weather, meant low water in the storm ball. A low-pressure system, the sort that heralded a storm, caused the water to rise and overflow the glass tube. Often called Dutch weather glasses or Liege barometers, storm balls were made chiefly by glass blowers in Liege, Belgium. In the 1800s, they were most often found on sailing ships and in the homes of ship captains and other mariners.

Long before being trapped in the bathing house, the mermaid had chanced to rescue a storm ball from a shipwreck. She kept the fragile instrument as a curiosity, never dreaming it would later be crucial to her well-being. Now a prisoner, she revered her storm ball for its powers of prediction. She knew as long as she kept it half-filled with water, it would show her when to be ready for the storm surge that would take her back out to sea.

So far, though, there had been many fierce thunderstorms, but no hurricane.

The mermaid was just about to lose hope when, late one sultry afternoon, the water began to rise up the glass tube. Though the ocean had been rougher than usual for two days, the mermaid barely raised an eyebrow, as she did not want to become excited over another false hope. Early that evening, when the water began to drip out the tip of the tube and the crashing of the waves grew louder, she bit her lip in an effort to hold back her rising expectations. Surely, her hopes were bound to be dashed again as she sat trapped alone in the darkness. She tried to quell her excitement as the wind rose and the rain intensified. All through the stormy night, she clutched her storm ball. One hand held the instrument upright while the other cupped the spout to catch the water that slowly seeped out.

As morning dawned, the mermaid peeped through the cracks in the siding of the bathing house. The gray sea was rougher than the day before, and the rising tide was already higher than even a lunar high tide. With increasing delight, she watched the tide lick ever closer. Soon, water was flowing under the door and across the plank floor of the bathing house before ebbing back again. With each ebb, she became increasingly confident that the returning flow would be higher.

Ebb, flow, ebb, flow—the tide slowly but steadily rose. The mermaid held her breath as a wave shook the door of the bathing house before ebbing back. When the next flow burst the padlocked wooden door open, she was ready. With one graceful sweep of her powerful tail, she was out the door and free!

Swimming steadily, the mermaid headed for the open ocean. A loud series of staccato cracks caused her to stop and turn to see what had happened. Her eyes widened as she saw the shake-shingled roof of the bathing house wrenched off by the force of a wave. Then the walls that had trapped her were burst open by the surging waves and pounded into an angry mix of torn lumber and bent nails.

Determined to avoid land and humans ever after, the mermaid dove at once to the ocean floor and swam far out to sea, free at last. With every swish of her tail, she swam farther from the people who had held her. She did not know that the sea raged higher than the highest lunar tide, crashing toward the big house where her captors huddled.

As the hurricane approached Magnolia Beach, the family

of Arthur Flagg, Jr., realized they had made a terrible mistake by remaining in their seaside home. All the servants working for the Flaggs had wanted to evacuate to Mrs. L. C. Hasell's nearby house on higher ground, but members of the Flagg family had told them it was not necessary.

Soon, the raging seawater surged too high for anyone to reach Mrs. Hasell's house. Too late, the Flagg family realized they should have evacuated. Now, they hoped only to live through the storm.

When the water surged into the lower level of their home, they sought refuge on the second story. When pieces of their house began to float by and chimney bricks were falling, they climbed out a window onto the roof of the porch and crossed to a nearby cedar tree. The Flaggs and all the servants clung to the branches as the raging sea battered them.

One by one, members of the Flagg family, their houseguests, and their servants were pulled from the tree. Arthur Flagg, Jr., his wife, and their five children drowned. His wife's visiting sisters, Alice and Elizabeth LaBruce, drowned, as did his wife's nieces, Elizabeth and Pauline Weston of Summerville. All the homes on Magnolia Beach were washed away except for the hill house of Mrs. L. C. Hasell.

Clinging to the tree for dear life, Dr. Ward Flagg was the only member of his family not swept away. All the household servants drowned except for Anthony Doctor. Anne Weston, another of Mrs. Flagg's nieces visiting from Summerville, lived through the storm surge by clinging to the same tree.

Forty years after the storm, Anne Weston described how she nearly gave in to the waves, winds, and floating debris that had torn away her sisters' hold. After twice losing and then regaining her grip on the small limb to which she clung, she felt there was no use to fight any longer.

Dr. Ward Flagg told her, "Live for your mother's sake." So fierce was the storm surge that she believed the tree had detached from the land and was being carried out to sea. Dr. Ward correctly told her it was still rooted.

The terrible storm brought on by the mermaid's incarceration caused the demise of most of the family in whose bathing house she had been held prisoner. But who had shut the child of the water in the dry, landlocked structure?

Why, a member of the Flagg family found her and shut her in there, according to Pauline Pyatt during a 1937 interview at the home of Georgetown resident Uncle Ben Horry.

"Dr. Ward shut that mere-maid up," recalled Pauline.

Between 1936 and 1938, as part of the Federal Writers' Project, Genevieve Chandler interviewed former slaves and children of former slaves living in the Waccamaw Neck area of Georgetown County. On June 15, 1937, she visited and interviewed Uncle Ben Horry, who was then over eighty years old. She also interviewed Pauline Pyatt, a guest of Uncle Ben's.

Ben described to Genevieve Chandler his vivid recollections of "the Flagg flood" forty-four years earlier. There on the porch of Ben's Murrells Inlet home, Pauline told of the mermaid, lured by bread, who was captured in September 1893 and held by the Flagg family in their seaside bathing house until the October storm set her free. The unnatural incarceration of the mermaid, Pauline inferred, caused the Flagg storm.

"Long as he have mere-maid shut up, it rain!" said Pauline, "People go there to look at 'em. Long as keep 'em shut up, it rain! That time, rain thirty days. That just 'fore Flagg storm."

The mermaid, Pauline explained, kept telling Dr. Arthur Flagg a storm was coming, and he would not believe her.

"Mermaid had a storm ball. . . . Keep a-telling him [Dr. Arthur] storm coming. He wouldn't believe 'em. He wouldn't believe."

She went on to describe the mermaid.

"Mere-maid got a forked tongue just like a shark. From here down, all blue scale like a catfish. Pretty people! Pretty a white woman as you ever lay your eye on.

"Dem stay in the sea. Dey walk—slide along on tail. . . . You got a bathing house on beach. Leave bread in there. They sho eat bread."

Uncle Ben added, "All that family drown because they wouldn't go to this lady's house on higher ground. Wouldn't let none of the rest go. Servant all drown! Betsy, Kit, Mom Adele! Dr. Wardie Flagg been saved hanging to a beach cedar."

Pauline remembered Dr. Ward's sadness over his family's demise in the terrible storm.

"I go there now and talk about that storm, and he eyes got full o' water," she said.

Dr. Ward Flagg continued to live at his home on Brookgreen Plantation, a few miles from where his family had perished. A beloved character of the Waccamaw Neck, he spent the rest of his life attending to the medical needs of all who needed his services, regardless of their ability to pay. When he died in 1938, two hundred African-Americans gathered to sing spirituals at his burial.

Had beloved Dr. Ward known the consequences of shutting the mermaid in the bathing house—by which he indirectly caused the Flagg flood and his family's deaths—he would no doubt have left her free to frolic in the ocean.

The Money Pit

Over the centuries, money has been the catalyst for greed, deceit, and murder. Nearly a century and a half ago, lust for money resulted in duplicity and death on a remote bank of the Sampit River. The ghosts of the men who were deceived that fateful night still haunt the river bend where they were murdered and buried.

Approximately twelve miles long, the Sampit is the shortest river in South Carolina. Its mouth is the entrance from Winyah Bay into the port of Georgetown. All vessels entering the port from the Atlantic must navigate Winyah Bay's shipping channel, then travel up the Sampit into Georgetown.

Soon after vessels enter the Sampit, Georgetown's infamous boat graveyard on uninhabited Goat Island lies to port. Once the site of a booming eighteenth-century lumberyard, tree-covered Goat Island is now a final resting place for eerie, mysterious, half-sunken relics of Georgetown's maritime past. Wooden shrimp trawlers, time-worn sailboats with masts still intact, hulking houseboat hulls, and ruined motor yachts give silent testament to their past glory days. Dark and still, they lie keeled over at the edge of the river despite periodic efforts to have them towed away.

Though the abandoned boats exude a ghostlike charm at the river entrance, the Sampit's ghost story does not lie here.

Front Street, which follows the first leg of the river, is to starboard. After winding past Georgetown's picturesque Harborwalk, specialty shops, fine restaurants, marinas, and commercial shrimp docks, the river reaches the State Ports Authority. Nearby are docked the gigantic steel-hulled oceangoing freighters that trade at Georgetown's river-front salt and steel industries. Red-and-black, deep-hulled ocean tugs dock nearby, ready to escort the huge freighters in from the ocean, nestle them up to the dock, and then take them out to sea again.

Up around the bend, the docks of the paper mill are lined with container barges brought by blue-and-white, flat-hulled river tugs. The river tugs push the great barges up and down the river and the nearby Intracoastal Waterway.

From the paper mill, the Sampit River heads inland. For ten miles, it winds through the Georgetown County countryside. Except for the modern docks of occasional homes and small marinas, this is a vista of nature and dark, dark water.

Breathtaking are the huge, high nests of eagles and ospreys.

Thrilling is a glimpse of a silently watching alligator.

The ghosts roam farther upriver, past the abandoned docks and shake-shingled edifices of a forgotten marina, at the bend near the railroad trestle. There, the ghosts of the

Money Pit dwell. They forever guard the spot on the riverbank where they were deceived and murdered—over money.

In February 1865, near the close of the Civil War, the town council of Georgetown formally surrendered to Federal officers. Georgetonians immediately began hiding their money and valuables. They feared Federal troops on their way north might stop to pillage and plunder.

Rice plantation owners along the Sampit River were especially fearful for their homes and treasures. After all, they reasoned, during the Revolutionary War nine decades earlier, had not British ships sailed right up the Sampit, burning the homes of Patriots? Now, Federal navy vessels were patrolling the harbor and could easily travel farther up the river.

One plantation owner, it is said, decided to bury his valuables—money, gold, silver, and jewelry. So bulky was his cache that, to hold it all, he piled it into a huge washtub. He was determined to keep his treasure safe at all costs.

According to local lore, he had two of his slaves take the washtub full of treasure to the riverbank, load it into a bateau, then row it across the river. The slaves were to bury it at the spot the plantation owner had marked on the other side, then row back across the river.

Dusk deepened on the chill, overcast February day as the slaves carefully rowed their heavy cargo across the river. They shook their heads each time a little water sloshed over the gunwale. The bateau sat far too low in the water, weighed down by the washtub. The return trip across the river promised to be much less tedious without the unwieldy burden. It was with great relief that the slaves finally felt the hull of the bateau thump on the shore. Now, they could bury their heavy load and row back home.

Unbeknownst to the slaves, the heartless plantation

owner did not expect them to return. He had hired two henchmen to make sure the secret of the treasure's location went with the slaves to their graves that very night.

Dutifully, the slaves found the appointed spot and hauled the washtub over to it. They dug a deep hole, as they had been instructed. By the time they finished, full dark had fallen. The night was inky and moonless, a heavy mist rising off the water. Their clandestine task, they thought, had been observed by no one.

The executioners rowed across the river as soon as darkness fell. Hidden by the night and the mist, their oars sliding carefully and silently through the murky water, they quickly reached the other side. Waiting quietly on the riverbank, they allowed time for the slaves to dig before approaching them.

Mist was rising from the river into the clammy air as the slaves lowered the washtub into the hole with long ropes. Muscles straining, they focused on keeping the washtub from tipping as it went down. As soon as it reached the bottom of the hole, the slaves relaxed their ropes and the henchmen stepped out of the shadows. Without hesitation, the henchmen fatally stabbed the two slaves. They then shoved them unceremoniously into the hole on top of the treasure-filled washtub. They had been instructed to dispose of the bodies elsewhere, but who was to know? After filling the hole, they covered the disturbed ground with leaves and sticks. Then they rowed back across the river to collect their fee.

The plantation owner, wearing a dark greatcoat, met them at the riverbank. He smiled as he noted the greedy anticipation on the henchmen's faces. Then he drew from the deep folds of his coat not a package of money but a double-barreled shotgun. At close range, he sent both henchmen to hell with one blast.

That done, the plantation owner assumed no one knew

the whereabouts of his treasure. Or did they?

When the plantation owner died a short time later, his secret did not perish with him. Whispered tales began to circulate of money and murder on the Sampit River. Two slaves, people said in hushed tones, had been murdered, their bodies thrown into a pit they had just finished digging. The burial spot contained untold wealth and was said to be haunted by the ghostly slave sentinels. By the early part of the twentieth century, the buried cache was known as the Money Pit.

But no one knew exactly where the Money Pit was.

The numerous plantations along the Sampit River had changed owners, acreages, and boundaries in the decades following the Civil War. Besides, no one knew for certain that the infamous plantation owner had buried the treasure on his own property. After all, it had been rowed away from his shore. According to legend, it had been rowed to his property across the river, but what if it had been taken downriver? Or upriver? Or to another property?

Seven decades after the war, during the Great Depression of the 1930s, a man who was "not from around here" came into possession of a portion of an old Sampit River plantation. The property had once belonged to the plantation owner remembered darkly for his Money Pit.

Foreclosures, tax sales, and property sales were frequent during that time. Many Georgetonians could not afford to keep their property. New owners from "away" were abundant, so this one drew little attention—until he made it known that he had found the Money Pit.

According to the man, he had heard the story of the Money Pit soon after acquiring the property. Later, a depression or sinkhole not far from the river had attracted his attention. Recalling the Money Pit story, he began to dig there. After much digging, he was about to give up when, lo and behold, his shovel struck something hard. He had found the legendary cache of treasure buried at the close of the Civil War, he said. But retrieving it, he went on, would be a problem. After over half a century in the damp, often-flooded riverbank, the washtub was no doubt as fragile as a spider web. The ground, he added, was unstable and prone to caving in.

And what *was* down there? Those whom the man took into his confidence always arrived at that inevitable question. The man would nod his head sagely, squint his eyes, and bestow a whispered phrase.

"Somethin' real shiny and bright-like" was how he described the wonders he had glimpsed in the Money Pit.

Excavating the pit, he confided, would be very costly. It might be awhile before he could raise enough capital for his private venture of bringing up the contents.

And private it was. The man would not let anyone know the exact location of his find. However, he was willing to accept investments in the expensive, time-consuming task of unearthing what was in the Money Pit. The rewards, he promised, would repay investors a hundredfold, a thousand-fold, maybe even more!

Despite the devastating economic conditions of the Great Depression, many investors wagered their last savings on the venture. After all, they said, it was quite legitimate, since people had known about the Money Pit for years. They just had not known where it was. Now, they knew its exact location—almost. Only the new landowner knew the exact spot where the Money Pit lay. He kept that secret safely to himself.

As the months passed, none of the investors let their faith in the forthcoming riches waver. The new owner was *so* trustworthy and kindhearted. He would not turn down anyone's investment, no matter how meager. His encouraging smile never failed to raise the hopes of the nearly impoverished as they trustingly handed over their family's milk money.

Despite many offers to visually assess the difficulty of

the excavation and numerous offers of help with the actual work, the new owner was a careful businessman. He shrewdly maintained his well-kept secret of the Money Pit's location.

And then the new landowner left. He told no one goodbye. One day, he was simply gone. Foul play was not suspected. A search of his home showed he had packed his bags and left town. He never came back to reclaim his land or the fortune buried on it. The land was not worth anywhere near the value of the fortune supposedly buried beneath it—or the fortune in investments the man had collected.

Had the landowner perpetrated a hoax and deliberately swindled his investors? Or had he truly found the Money Pit and chosen to run off with the investments instead of excavating his find? Or had he dug up the Money Pit and run off with the investments *and* the treasure?

Many of the disappointed and frustrated investors refused to believe the man would leave behind the fabulous wealth legend held was in the Money Pit. Surely, some ill fate had befallen him. Fearing him dead, some of the investors began to search his land.

At a sharp bend across from a tiny island way up the river, they made an exciting discovery. A great hole had been dug in the woods just out of sight of the riverbank.

The Money Pit! In the owner's absence, they would have to excavate it themselves. They dug and dug, but every time they touched what felt like something hard, the pit filled with water and caved in. Despite the walls of heavy timber placed in the pit to shore it up, the sides collapsed every time the diggers reached a considerable depth.

At the height of the investors' fevered excavating, a hurricane came and changed forever that bend in the river as ocean water flooded the brackish Sampit. When the wind finally ceased and the flood of salt water at last receded, the Money Pit was nowhere to be seen. The subterranean wall of timber was washed away. The tiny island marking the spot was gone. The sharp bend in the river had been reconfigured to a gentler curve. The trees around the Money Pit, as well as all trees close to the riverbank, began to slowly die from being inundated by salt water. The Money Pit itself was completely filled in. The amount of hurricane-scattered debris around the excavation site made it indistinguishable from any other area on the devastated riverside.

The investors who believed the landowner had met with foul play shook their heads sadly. Other investors—those who believed he had deliberately run off with their money—shook their fists angrily.

Boaters who plied the waters of the Sampit on damp, cold winter afternoons when dusk was beginning to settle and the mist started to rise off the water sometimes saw an eerie sight as they came around a gentle bend in the river. Two ethereal forms floating in diaphanous weightlessness would rise out of the woods close by the riverbank and slowly and steadily make their way across the water to the other side. Then they would fade into the mist.

The phantoms that traversed the river, it was whispered, were the murdered slaves who had dug the Money Pit and were buried in it. Some believed the slaves' ghosts were guiding the way to the treasure. Others felt the eerie sentinels were protecting the Money Pit for all time. Still others swore that, rather than guarding the treasure, the slaves' ghosts were forever leaving their hidden grave to seek the liberty they deserved.

Anyone who may have known the secret of the Money Pit has long since passed away. The long-ago murdered slaves, their freedom a greater treasure than any earthly valuable, will always hold the key to the mystery.

The Sampit Drawbridge Tragedy

Another tragedy took place on the Sampit River many years after the Money Pit was first dug. While the saga of the Money Pit left a legacy of ghosts, mystery, and treasure, the Sampit drawbridge tragedy broke hearts and created an enduring mystery that may never be solved.

One fateful August night in 1931, a terrible drawbridge accident took the lives of twenty-three Georgetown County people returning from a beach outing. Despite detailed investigation, no one is sure exactly what happened. The cause of the tragedy remains a mystery.

The modern Sylvan L. Rosen Bridge crosses the Sampit River to link the Maryville neighborhood with the rest of Georgetown. The twin spans of the tall bridge allow boats to pass beneath unheeded. It is difficult to picture, in the same place, a single flat drawbridge that was raised, then lowered every time a boat required passage. Yet in 1931, a drawbridge was part of everyday life for those who regularly crossed the Sampit.

The Sampit drawbridge was a single-leaf bascule bridge. Bascule is the French word for seesaw or balance, the principle upon which most drawbridges work. A bascule bridge consists of either one or two spans, or leaves. Each leaf has a center weight that continuously balances the span throughout the raise, or draw. Instead of having two leaves that opened in the center, the Sampit drawbridge had a single leaf that hinged on the north bank of the river and opened on the south bank.

The draw was closed most of the time. Drivers could usually take their vehicles over the drawbridge without having to wait for it to close. During those times when the draw was open, gates on either side of the drawbridge were closed. Closing the gates prevented vehicles traveling south, from the Georgetown side, from hitting the raised leaf and kept vehicles traveling north, from the Maryville side, from continuing forty feet to the riverbank and plunging into the river below. Vehicles had to wait behind the closed gates for the drawbridge to lower and the gates to open. Still, waiting for the drawbridge to close in 1931 was a far cry from a decade earlier, when all traffic had to wait to be carried across on a ferry.

On the night of Monday, August 3, 1931, a driver traveling north on Route 40 failed to stop in time for the closed gate on the Maryville—or south—side of the open drawbridge. He was driving a rented school bus. The bus crashed through the gate, traveled forty feet to the riverbank, then plunged into the Sampit. The result was one of the most tragic accidents in the county's history.

Why did the driver not stop at the closed gate? And

why could he not stop in the forty feet between the gate and the river?

That morning, five rented school buses filled with men, women, and children had left Andrews for a day of picnicking at Riverside Beach near Mount Pleasant. At the end of the picnic, the buses departed Riverside Beach for the return trip to Andrews at approximately 8:45 P.M.

Later that evening, after the first three buses drove safely across the Sampit River drawbridge, the gates were closed so the draw could be opened. While the draw was open and the gates closed, the fourth and fifth buses approached. The fourth bus did not slow down as it neared the barricaded drawbridge but rather broke through the gate and plunged into the river, which was thirty-six feet deep at that point. Of the twenty-four people on the bus, only one survived. Eighteen-year-old Jerome Fraser swam to the fender of the drawbridge, where bridge tender C. E. Richardson and his helper, Willie Lambert, pulled him out.

The drawbridge was closing as the fifth bus arrived. It picked up Fraser, took him into Georgetown for emergency treatment of his cut hand, then continued to Andrews.

News of the accident reached Andrews before the buses did. Family members of the riders of all five buses gathered to await the news of who was aboard the ill-fated fourth bus. When the fifth and last bus, carrying Fred Green, organizer of the picnic, arrived in Andrews, Green completed a check of his passenger lists. He determined who had been riding the fourth bus.

Efforts to raise the bus began immediately after the accident and lasted through the night. At 5 A.M. Tuesday, the sunken bus was raised and floated down the river to Georgetown. Dragging the river also began immediately after the accident. It continued until 8:45 A.M. Wednesday, when the last body was found.

Eleven men, nine women, and three children had

drowned. The victims ranged in age from two to fifty-three. All of the victims were black with the exception of the white bus owner and his son.

An estimated five thousand people visited the Sampit drawbridge Tuesday as friends and relatives of the victims waited during recovery operations. An unidentified white woman shouting "I want to drown myself here!" had to be restrained by her companion and a bridge tender as she fought to throw herself off the drawbridge and into the river Tuesday night.

An inquest was held the day after the accident by Magistrate O. M. Higgins. Giving testimony were bridge tender C. E. Richardson, Richardson's helper, Willie Lambert, and the survivor, Jerome Fraser—the only three people to witness the accident. Also testifying were Fred Green, organizer of the trip, and J. S. Bourne, who had participated in salvage operations.

In his sworn testimony at the inquest, Richardson said, "Last night about 11 o'clock, I had an occasion to open the draw to let a boat pass through. There are gates to be shut at each end about 40 feet from the draw. I closed and fastened the gates and then opened the draw. When the gates are closed there is a sign on each gate that would be facing the approach to the draw. They were on there last night. After I had closed the gates and had the draw almost open there was a truck coming towards Georgetown. I could see the truck coming around the curve and would judge [it] to be running about 40 miles per hour. The driver did not stop but hit the gates. Knocked it open and went right in overboard. [I] did not see the truck slow up or anything, but [it] came right on and went into the river. When the truck went overboard this young man popped up and hollered for help. I called Mr. Lambert to bring the boat. Lambert brought the boat, but the boy swam to the fenders of the bridge, and I climbed down the fenders and got him by the hand and helped him on the bridge. I have been bridge tender for about three years, and this gate has been knocked open twice before this night. The other gate has been knocked open once. These gates are fastened with a pin, and when hit, the pin jumps out. I am employed by the State Highway Department. I called the Highway Department's attention each time that the gates were broken open."

Funerals for the victims were held in Andrews and at Bethel A.M.E. Church in Georgetown. The local undertakers did not have enough hearses to handle all of the services in such a short period, so a number of caskets were carefully carried on trucks. Mourners came from all over the state, as well as from North Carolina, Massachusetts, Ohio, and New York.

Today, U.S. 17 traces the path once run by Route 40 from Charleston to Georgetown. Few reminders exist of the old drawbridge that once crossed the Sampit River, save those twenty-three graves in cemeteries throughout the county.

Accidental drowning was determined to be the cause of death for all of the victims. Despite careful investigation, it remains a mystery why the bus crashed through the guard gate, then traveled forty more feet to plunge into the river. A rumor suggested the bus owner's son had imbibed so frequently from a bottle in his pocket that his driving was impaired as he piloted the bus toward Georgetown that fateful night.

Was that the reason?

We may never know.

Cinthy

Some of Georgetown's ghosts have made their eerie appearances for many years due to a fate not understood, a problem unresolved, or a search not fulfilled.

Other ghosts have haunted for a brief period of time, then ceased to appear once their objectives were met. The situations causing the ghosts to materialize were either resolved or altered enough for the appearances to no longer be necessary.

Such was the case with the ghost of Cinthy, witnessed night after night by two little boys named Robert and Jesse. Cinthy came back to ask the boys for possessions she had left behind. After they assisted her to the best of their ability, they never saw her again.

The saga of Robert and Jesse began in 1899, when they were orphaned at ages four and six, respectively. Feared by

many, the two orphans were wanted by no one except struggling plantation owner and writer Elizabeth Allston Pringle.

Born in 1845, Pringle was in her mid-teens when the
War Between the States began. She grew up on Chicora
Wood Plantation in a family that owned many slaves. By
the war's end, her father had passed away, her mother was in
charge of the plantation, and the former slaves were free.
Many of them chose to remain at Chicora Wood and work
for wages.

Pringle soon married and went to live at her husband's
family's rice plantation, White House. They had been married less than a decade when they lost the plantation and
her husband died of malaria. She somehow managed to buy
back White House, determined to make it profitable. When
her mother died, Pringle had very little money and the responsibility of two rice plantations, White House and
Chicora Wood.

Many of the former slaves and children of former slaves
living and working on Pringle's plantations now looked to
her for numerous needs, including medical attention.

One September morning in 1899, Pringle visited a young
man in whose hands gunpowder had exploded. After tend-
ing his wounds, she was summoned to the home of a sick
widow. Though Pringle rushed to her side, the woman was
mortally ill. Unable to save her life, Pringle promised to
care for her young sons, Robert and Jesse.

Pringle was at first supplanted by the widow's mother,
who took her orphaned grandsons home with her. Pringle
promised the grandmother that she would provide whatever was needed for the boys. A few months later, however,
the grandmother announced that she did not want to keep
Robert and Jesse. They were bad, she said, like their father
had been.

Pringle loaded the boys into her wagon and took them
home with her, much to the distress of the former slaves

and their children who lived and worked at her home. Chloe, Pringle's close friend and servant, explained that Robert and Jesse, as foreigners, should not be brought into their midst.

Chloe's feelings mirrored those of the other African-Americans on the plantation. Robert and Jesse, very small for their ages, were said to be half-pygmy heathens because of their father. Nearly all of the African-Americans on Pringle's plantation had been there for generations and were descended from the same African tribes. But Robert and Jesse's father had come directly from Africa and was believed by the local African-Americans to be from a different tribe—a pygmy tribe. Though he had married one of their own people, the other African-Americans insisted he was from a different part of Africa and from a wicked tribe.

Nevertheless, Pringle brought Robert and Jesse home and installed them in one of the two bedrooms in the old washhouse. Immediately, the cook and poultry keeper, Goody, who had the other bedroom, announced she could not live next to Robert and Jesse. They were too dirty, Goody said. Even after the boys were thoroughly bathed and re-dressed and their old clothes were burned, she remained indignant. She gave Pringle her notice after a few days and was soon gone.

Chloe took over the cooking, but Pringle did not want her to be responsible for the poultry keeping, too. So she hired Cinthy, a woman from another plantation, to take care of the poultry. Cinthy would live in the other bedroom in the washhouse, next to Robert and Jesse.

Cinthy owned very little and badly needed the job. She was delighted with her new position and living quarters. Not only did she not mind occupying the room next to Robert and Jesse, she was happy to do so.

Robert and Jesse were equally glad to have Cinthy in the room next to them. They sang hymns and sat contentedly before the fire after she moved in. Though Cinthy was only middle-aged, the boys began to call her "Aunt," a term of endearment usually reserved for the oldest ladies on the plantation.

One afternoon, Pringle brought Cinthy a new pair of shoes in the very small size Cinthy had requested. Cinthy declined to try them on, saying she would wait until morning, after she had washed her feet.

The next morning, Pringle heard that Cinthy was not feeling well. She got a mug of coffee and took it to Cinthy's room. She found Cinthy kneeling by her bed praying. Pringle set the coffee on the hearth and sat down near the fire to wait. Soon, Cinthy became quiet. Thinking she had fallen asleep, Pringle went over and placed her hand on Cinthy's shoulder. Cinthy was gone. She had passed away while saying her prayers. Her new shoes, never worn, were on the floor by her knees.

Pringle summoned the doctor. Cinthy, he explained, had suffered from a heart condition no one knew about, not even Cinthy herself.

Pringle had a carpenter build a coffin and made the lining herself. She gave a long white gown of her own for Cinthy to be laid out and buried in and also found a black ribbon to make a bow for the deceased. Cinthy was buried in the plantation's old slave cemetery, where former slaves were now laid to rest.

Cinthy's son, who had come from Georgetown for the funeral, said he did not want any of his mother's possessions. Pringle gave Cinthy's friends the few items the deceased had owned. She set aside Cinthy's new shoes for the time when someone else would need them. No one wanted Cinthy's bedframe, so Pringle had it taken to the orchard, where it could slowly weather into the ground.

Fearing that Robert and Jesse would feel uncomfortable staying alone in their room next to Cinthy's empty abode, Pringle arranged for them to stay with one of the men on the plantation. To her surprise, the boys did not want to leave their quarters in the washhouse. Not only did they have no qualms about sleeping next door to Cinthy's empty room, they soon asked to move into it. Already spotless, the room had been newly cleaned and whitewashed after Cinthy's passing. Pringle agreed. Soon, Robert and Jesse were happily ensconced in Cinthy's former room.

Over a year went by.

Jesse attended the nearby school and Robert, too young for school, kept busy on the plantation. Usually well behaved when apart, the boys were fearless and bold together. As a team, they seemed daunted by nothing. They found mischief anywhere they could and created their own when none was available. Neither the dark of night nor anything in its inky folds caused the boys a moment of trepidation—until they began having a nocturnal visitor.

Chloe asked Pringle if the boys had spoken to her about anything.

No, Pringle replied. Spoken to her about what?

Chloe declined to elaborate and urged Pringle to question the boys.

Privately, Pringle asked Jesse if he had seen anything.

Without faltering even an instant, he replied that he had seen Aunt Cinthy.

Though Pringle assured him Cinthy was in heaven and would not wish to come back down even if she were able, Jesse insisted he had seen her. Aunt Cinthy had called him, he said, when he was sleeping. He had opened his eyes to find her standing before him. Dressed in white with a black ribbon bow, she had gazed very pointedly at him.

Jesse had asked her what she wanted, and she replied, "I want my bed. Give me my bed."

Jesse informed Cinthy that he did not have her bed.

"Where is my bed?" she persisted.

"Your bed is in the orchard," Jesse replied.

Cinthy continued to stare at Jesse. "I want my shoe. Give me my shoe," she said.

"I don't have your shoe," Jesse replied.

"Give me my five cents. I want my five cents," Cinthy went on.

Jesse replied, "I never saw your five cents. Go away and leave me alone."

After listening to his vivid account, Pringle assured Jesse that it was all a dream, that Cinthy could not come back and would not even if she could.

Without wasting any time, Pringle quickly found Robert and asked him a question that would give him an opening to tell of ghostly nocturnal occurrences—or not.

Robert immediately lit into a narration of the ghostly visit of Cinthy. Just as Jesse had, Robert described Cinthy as clothed in white with a black bow. His version of the visitation was identical to Jesse's.

Pringle decided not to mention the incident to the boys again, in case their talking to her about it made it more vivid in their minds. Perhaps it would cease to be foremost in the boys' thoughts if not much was made over Cinthy's alleged visit.

After a week, Chloe came to find Pringle. She told her that Cinthy was harrying the boys. Chloe felt at fault for Cinthy's visits. While clearing Cinthy's room before the burial, Chloe had found five cents tied in a burlap bag attached to the head of the deceased's bedframe. One of Cinthy's friends had asked for the five cents to place in the collection plate at church, and Chloe had given it to her. Dejectedly, Chloe told Pringle she wished she had put the five cents in Cinthy's hand and made sure it was buried with her. That way, Cinthy would not now be coming back to find it.

No one but Chloe and Cinthy's friend had known about the five cents. But Robert and Jesse insisted Cinthy had come into the room and asked for it!

Chloe went on to relate that Jesse said Cinthy called him every night at the time the first cock crowed, during that darkest period just before dawn. Sometimes, she called Robert also. Chloe suggested that burning sulfur in the room would cause Cinthy to rest and her visits to cease.

Several days later, Jim, one of the men on the plantation, came to Pringle and told her he wished she would "do something" about Robert and Jesse. He said the boys had been sleeping for five nights in the hayloft over the horse stable. Cinthy, he went on, had run the boys out of their room so thoroughly that they refused to go back and stay in their house at all.

Chloe had even more to relate. Jesse, she informed Pringle, had been born with a birth caul over his head. A child born in that manner, she reminded Pringle, grew up to see spirits unless the mother made him swallow the caul. Jesse's mother, said Chloe, had thrown away the caul, thus resigning Jesse to a lifetime of seeing spirits.

Unanswered was the unspoken question—why did Robert, too, see Cinthy? Had he also been born with a caul over his head? Or was Cinthy's ghostly presence so intense that she was visible to anyone in the room?

Pringle thought back to the narrations Robert and Jesse had provided of Cinthy's ghostly questions and requests. "I want my bed. Give me my bed" had been Cinthy's first words upon appearing to the boys. She had also asked for her shoes and her five cents, but the bed seemed to be her main reason for haunting Robert and Jesse. Pringle shared this information with Jim. She suggested a solution to the problem, emphasizing that Robert and Jesse take part.

A short time later, Jim, though reluctant, promised that he, Robert, and Jesse would go to the orchard and retrieve Cinthy's bed. They would carry it to the cemetery and place it over Cinthy's grave. They would not attempt to return the shoes or the five cents.

Once that was done, Robert and Jesse happily moved back into their room in the washhouse.

Though Pringle lived for two more decades, she never heard of any more appearances by Cinthy.

Elizabeth Allston Pringle is remembered today as an author. Like many female authors of her day, she wrote under an assumed name. Hers was Patience Pennington. She published the autobiographical *A Woman Rice Planter* under her pseudonym in 1913. In the book, she detailed the adventures, joys, and hardships of a woman with nearly no money running two rice plantations. *Chronicles of Chicora Wood*, concerning her ancestral rice plantation, was published a year after her 1921 death.

Rab and Dab, handwritten by Pringle near the turn of the twentieth century, was published as a magazine serial in 1903 and in hardcover over eighty years later. *Rab and Dab* is the true account of Robert and Jesse Spivy. For the purpose of her book, Pringle renamed Robert and Jesse as Rab and Dab, after the biblical nomads Rabinadab and Abinadab. Robert and Jesse, she explained, were homeless nomads like their biblical counterparts.

Frolic

Never name a vessel after one that has shipwrecked or sunk.

This is not merely a suggestion but a powerful maritime superstition. For that reason, vessels with the same moniker as their lost predecessors often have the Roman numeral II, III, or IV after their names.

A violent shipwreck at the entrance to Georgetown Harbor on Thanksgiving Day 1996 sank the newly built thirty-five-foot wooden schooner *Frolic* on her maiden voyage as she sailed down the coast from New Hampshire. Her owner, sailing alone, was never found.

The tragedy appears unrelated to past maritime events until one considers the eerily similar shipwreck of an eerily similar vessel with the same name in another ocean nearly a century and a half earlier.

Was the similarity coincidental? Or was the fate of the new schooner *Frolic* sealed when she was given the same name as a larger schooner that shipwrecked and sank in 1850?

Though other vessels have borne the name *Frolic*, the

parallels between the two schooners are uncanny. The *Frolic* that shipwrecked in 1850 was a wooden-hulled Chesapeake Bay Baltimore clipper schooner. Only five years old, she was on her first voyage to San Francisco when she shipwrecked off the northern California coast, ramming a rocky reef off Point Cabrillo.

The *Frolic* that shipwrecked in 1996 was a wooden-hulled sailing vessel custom-designed in the style of a Chesapeake Bay schooner. Less than a year old, she was on her maiden voyage when she shipwrecked off the South Carolina coast, crashing into the granite rocks of the north jetty at the entrance to Georgetown Harbor. Each of the vessels was under full sail at night and sank quickly when she suffered her deadly collision. And the captain of each of the vessels was involved in her design and construction—and remained her only captain from her inception to her sinking.

When her keel was laid in 1844, the *Frolic* already had a captain and a purpose. She was custom-built for the Boston firm Augustine Heard & Company to run opium from Bombay to Hong Kong. Instead of having the *Frolic* built at a local shipyard, A. Heard & Co. hired Baltimore shipbuilders William and George Gardiner, as Baltimore was a focal point for the construction of fast ships that could carry large cargoes. Captain Edward Horatio Faucon was captain of the *Frolic* from her construction. During the design phase, he was the one who made all decisions regarding her rigging.

Launched in 1845, the *Frolic* was highly successful as an opium trader until the British East India Company began using steamships for transporting opium. By 1847, the savings of using steamships over clipper ships was $1.28 per chest. The British East India Company then flooded the China opium market with its less expensively purchased opium. As a result, the *Frolic* and other clipper ships were obsolete for the opium trade. What commercial venture was next?

Captain Faucon, still master of the *Frolic*, was competitive and adventurous. A. Heard & Co. gave him a change of destination. Now, instead of bringing opium to China, he carried exotic goods from Hong Kong to nourish the tastes of the gold-rush boom town of San Francisco. The *Frolic* was loaded with a grand cargo of Chinese goods—silk fans, brass weights for shopkeepers to measure their wares, candied fruits, tortoise-shell combs, toothbrushes, ivory napkin rings, silver tinderboxes, porcelain bowls, mother-of-pearl gaming pieces, exquisite silks, finely detailed trunks, marble-topped tables, jewelry, and even a prefabricated two-room house with oyster-shell windows. The sole non-Chinese cargo was over a thousand bottles of ale from Edinburgh.

Tuesday, July 25, 1850

After sailing six thousand miles across the Pacific on a forty-four-day passage from Hong Kong, the *Frolic* was traveling off the northern California coast. By the light of the full moon, the mountains twenty miles in the distance were very clear. The fog just ahead, however, hid the low coastal terrace and the offshore rocks of a dangerous reef.

The first officer saw the reef and rushed to tell Captain Faucon, who turned the wheel instantly to port. It was too late. As the *Frolic*'s stern crashed into a rock, a huge gash was torn in her hull and her rudder broke off.

All twenty-six of the *Frolic*'s crew survived the initial impact. Six men, however, would not leave the ship to board the two lifeboats. Those half-dozen stayed up in the ship's rigging. Captain Faucon and the rest of the crew rowed the two boats to the mouth of the Big River, where the captain explored two miles into the interior without finding anyone. At that point, some of the crew, now safely on land, did not want to get back into their rowboat, as it was leaking badly. Those crew members chose to travel for help by land, while Captain Faucon and the others used the intact rowboat to row to the town of Bodega, north of San Francisco. From there, they slept on the beaches and ate mussels until they reached San Francisco. No one knows what became of the crew members who stayed in the rigging of the *Frolic* or those who chose to separate from Captain Faucon and travel by land.

The day he arrived in San Francisco, Captain Faucon was interviewed by the *Daily Alta California*. The following day, the paper reported his arrival and his estimated value of the *Frolic's* cargo of Chinese merchandise at $150,000.

The *Frolic* lay on the ocean floor off Point Cabrillo for many years, the only known wreck site of a Baltimore clipper. Captain Faucon went on to serve the Union during the Civil War and later made his fortune in the salvage business. He never forgot the terrible evening when he shipwrecked on a rocky reef at night in the great schooner *Frolic*.

Nearly a century and a half later, the 1996-built *Frolic*, a thirty-five-foot likeness of the ninety-seven-foot ship, met the same fate on Georgetown Harbor's north jetty.

Built in the late 1800s, the north jetty stretches from the tip of North Island way out into the Atlantic. The south jetty, built next, runs parallel to the north jetty, extending into the Atlantic from South Island. Between the jetties is the entrance to the shipping channel that leads into Winyah Bay and connects Georgetown Harbor with the Atlantic.

Constructed to keep a sand bar from building up at the channel entrance, the jetties were made of hundreds of great granite rocks. Each stone, some the size of boulders, was brought by train from upper South Carolina to Georgetown. The stones were then taken by tugboat to North Island, where the jetty construction was based.

After construction of the jetties, the sand bar that had

prevented deep-draft ships from accessing Georgetown Harbor was no longer a hazard to navigation. In conjunction with diligent dredging, the jetties kept the channel deep enough for giant freighters to reach Georgetown Harbor from the Atlantic.

But while the jetties remedied the hazard to navigation posed by the sand bar, their construction created another hazard—two rock walls stretching out into the ocean. The north and south jetties form a jagged silhouette against the horizon at low tide. At high tide, however, when the jetties are nearly covered, more than one vessel has crashed into the jagged boulders.

That was the fate of the 1996 *Frolic*.

Wednesday, November 27, 1996, Thanksgiving Eve

The *Frolic* and her captain were on a night passage down the southern half of the South Carolina coast. The open Atlantic lay to port. To starboard lay the bays, inlets, channels, and wide, sandy beaches of the Palmetto State.

The *Frolic* had already passed one of the trickiest and most dangerous legs of her journey down the East Coast. Her captain, who was also her sole crew member, had successfully navigated the treacherous seas off the Outer Banks of North Carolina, a literal ship graveyard legendary for the many vessels wrecked over hundreds of years on the treacherous shoals and rocks. The sail down the South Carolina coast, which had fewer hazards to navigation, was relaxing by comparison.

Following the coastline at high tide, the captain kept the *Frolic* on an eastward path close along the shore of North Island. Hidden ahead in the darkness were the huge, unyielding rocks of the island's granite jetty.

Sometime during the early morning of November 28,

the *Frolic* slammed into the north jetty. The impact tore a two-foot gash in her port side.

At about eight that morning, the thirty-five-foot schooner was found partly submerged in the Atlantic at the entrance to Georgetown Harbor near the north jetty rocks, the huge gash in her bright green hull a harsh testimony to her crash. Her sails were up, indicating that the crash was unexpected and that she was probably traveling fast. A small amount of debris and four life vests were discovered floating around her. No one was found aboard or nearby.

By Monday, the home port and owner registration of the *Frolic* were still a mystery. Where did she hail from? To whom did she belong? Who had been aboard?

The seas were rough. The water around the jetties, which create deep tidal swells on the calmest of days, was even more turbulent. Underwater visibility was meager. Divers could determine little about the wooden-hulled sailing vessel except that she seemed to be new and well maintained and was named the *Frolic*.

In a front-page article on the accident and search, the *Georgetown Times* reported that the *Frolic* had last been spotted near Oak Island, North Carolina, with apparently one man on board. Was he aboard when the *Frolic* crashed into the north jetty? Or had he fallen or been knocked overboard miles earlier?

One week later, the *Times* reported that the owner of the *Frolic* had been identified as Reginald L. Butler of Portsmouth, New Hampshire. This discovery was made after Captain Ronnie Campbell led a dive on the wreck during which two divers detected a hull number in the boat's companionway. That discovery led to the identification of the *Frolic*'s owner.

The 1996 *Frolic* was, like her predecessor, a Chesapeake Bay–style deadrise or deep-V-hull schooner. Baltimore clippers such as the 1845 *Frolic* were modified Chesapeake Bay coastal trading schooners. The Baltimore clipper class of ships, with their sharp-lined hulls and billowing sails, were perhaps the most beautiful sailing vessels ever built. The word *clipper* accurately described the speed of the sleek schooners, whose deep draft enabled them to sail closer to the wind than other vessels.

Butler's 1996 *Frolic* was built at the Landing School of Boatbuilding and Design in Arundel, Kennebunkport, Maine. Boatbuilding faculty at the school did not recall that Reginald Butler ever mentioned designing his boat as a replica of the ill-fated 1845 *Frolic*. But they did remember that Reg, as they fondly called him, was very active in the design of his schooner.

"Reg did not model his boat after the older *Frolic*," shared a member of the faculty. "It was modeled after his mind's eye from the guy who helped build it as a Chesapeake Bay deadrise-type boat."

Unintentional though it may have been, Butler's custom-designed 1996 schooner emerged as a one-third-scale ringer of the 1845 *Frolic*.

"But whether Butler was actually on the 35 foot wooden sailboat when it sank," reported Kelly M. Burch of the *Times*, "is still in question, according to Coast Guard officers in Georgetown and Miami. Butler's body was not found on the boat by divers from a private salvage company Wednesday morning.

"It is speculated that Butler may have hired someone to pilot the *Frolic* to another port in Florida or loaned the vessel to a friend. Butler has not been reported missing. The Coast Guard was attempting to contact his family members Wednesday morning to discover his whereabouts."

"Nobody has heard from him, but nobody has reported him missing," said Chief Petty Officer Mark Dobson with the Charleston Coast Guard Station. "We're presuming he was going from New Hampshire to Florida for the winter.

"His residence in Portsmouth was closed off and boarded up for the winter," Dobson said. "A lot of people from up north bring their boats down for the winter and take them back in the spring. But usually somebody on the other end is waiting for their arrival."

A short time later, Captain Campbell pulled the *Frolic* away from the jetty, out of the ocean, through Winyah Bay, and into the mouth of the Sampit River, grounding her at East Bay Street Landing in Georgetown. The once-beautiful *Frolic* lay aground, the gash in her port side now large enough to walk through. Irreparable, she waited to be broken up. Little was salvageable.

The search for Butler's body continued, to no avail. Besides the Thanksgiving disappearance of Butler, several Georgetown residents perished at sea and in local waters during November and December, also resulting in massive searches.

About a month later, according to Burch, the *Frolic's* dinghy was found near Bull Island, some thirty-five miles south of the jetty on which the *Frolic* crashed.

Sometime after the shipwreck, the owners of Georgetown's waterfront River Room Restaurant requested the bow of the *Frolic* for the restaurant's extensive collection of maritime antiques and local historic nautical memorabilia. They mounted the bow in a place of honor facing east toward the Sampit River, Winyah Bay, and the Atlantic.

But what of Butler?

His schooner, like her nineteenth-century predecessor, met her demise on ocean-covered rocks close to shore but far from her destination. Did Butler die here, too? Or had he fallen or been knocked overboard by the rigging miles prior, leaving his vessel to sail unmanned onto the jetty rocks? And why was his dinghy found so far ahead of his wreck?

"None of his people came down after the accident to see what happened," said Captain Campbell. "There are some things we will never know.

"There are other boats named *Frolic*," he added, "and when I see one, that wreck always comes to mind."

Remember—*never name a vessel after one that has shipwrecked or sunk.*

Drunken Jack the Pirate

While pirates have sailed the open seas for hundreds of years, the golden age of piracy lasted from 1713 to 1725.

During that time, pirates constantly roamed the Carolina coast, making frequent landfalls at bustling seaports as well as in sheltered coastal havens. Since Georgetown lies between the major seaports of Wilmington and Charleston and is bordered by secluded inlets, its coast was a prime location for pirate activity. Murrells Inlet, on Georgetown County's northern coast, and North Inlet, on its southern coast, each provided a secluded deepwater cove where pirate ships could lie in wait, ready to make chase when they sighted British vessels. In fact, Murrells Inlet was named for Captain John Morrall, a pirate who made his home in the inlet for just that purpose.

It was beside a small, uninhabited island in the Murrells Inlet vicinity that one pirate ship anchored to bury a recently stolen cache of excellent Caribbean rum. Far too much to drink at once, and much too fine to trade or risk being stolen, the cases of rum needed to be hidden for future consumption. Anchored in the calm water off the island, the pirates offloaded case after case into their ship's dinghy, rowed to shore to offload again, then rowed back to the ship for more. Over and over they repeated the process until all the rum was on the island.

This was their first landfall since procuring the rum, so the pirates were eager to spend some time on dry land sampling their newly acquired and highly intoxicating potion. Energetic with the feel of land beneath their sea legs, they divided up their duties and busied themselves burying the cases of rum, making a great bonfire, and gathering fine inlet oysters. The pungent aromas of roasting oysters and full-bodied dark rum blended with the salt air. One of the pirates brought out his bodrahn and began to beat out a rhythm as a shipmate piped a merry melody on his fife. Another pirate brought a penny whistle out of his vest and began to play along. Others joined in, singing one well-seasoned sea chantey after another.

A cool breeze blew in from the Atlantic across the long, sandy point that partially hid and mostly protected the inlet from the Atlantic. As the sun set, the evening took on a soothing, mystical feel. This was a night of relaxation and peace for the wiser, more well-rounded pirates. But others, never satisfied, felt the need to intensify the evening's pleasure with more and more rum.

One pirate, Jack, loved rum dearly and drank until he was in a complete stupor. His last conscious thought was how pleasant the cool sand felt against his cheek as he nestled under the low-hanging fronds of a bush palmetto.

The next morning when Jack awoke, he was reluctant to open his eyes because his head hurt so much. A cool, gentle breeze caressed his cheek. All was quiet except for the calling of the sea gulls and the distant lap of the ocean on the point, both of which were too loud for Jack's throbbing head. Finally, he opened his eyes.

He was lying on his side and apparently had not moved all night, for the bottle in his hand was standing upright with rum still in it. Holding his head with his other hand, Jack sat up. He squeezed his eyes shut to stop the spinning and to block the sunlight and bright water. Even with his eyes closed, his mind's eye could still see the blinding glare of the water and the sun. The picture should have held something else, though. Jack opened his eyes. The glare of the water should have been broken by his ship riding at anchor. The voices of his shipmates should have been heard all across the small island. Jack leaped up, his throbbing head forgotten. He looked wildly all around.

He was alone.

Late that afternoon, off the coast of North Carolina, one of the crew approached the captain.

"Sir, none has seen Jack since last evenin'."

The captain raised one eyebrow in surprise and lowered the other in concern.

"The last anybody seen, he was a-sleepin' off by himself," the crew member continued.

"Humph." The captain ran his hand over his bearded chin. He shook his head. "We canna go back. We'll fetch Jack on the downhill run. He'll fare fine."

The next day, the ship was nearly captured outside Wilmington and headed south. Her course, however, did not take her down the coast past Murrells Inlet. The pirates kept a southerly heading far out to sea to avoid capture.

It was over a year before they returned to the island where they had accidentally left Jack. Their purpose in returning was twofold—to fetch Jack and to recover their buried rum. They were able to fulfill neither quest.

When the ship anchored near the island, the pirate crew

thought Jack had found a way off and was long gone. He was nowhere to be seen. After going ashore, however, they made a gruesome discovery. All that remained of Jack was a bleached skeleton. It was a breezy day, and the wind made a soft whistling sound as it blew through his sun-whitened bones.

And the rum?

Jack, who so loved rum, had been left with nothing else to drink. He had dug up and drunk the entire cache. Bottles were strewn up and down the shore.

Jack's bleached bones and empty bottles are long gone, but his ghost remains on what has come to be known as Drunken Jack Island. His ghost is occasionally seen there, hovering near the shore holding a bottle.

And sometimes, on windy days, it is possible to hear the distinct sound of the wind softly whistling through his bleached bones.

South Island

Georgetown County is legendary for its ghosts. While none of the apparitions are threatening, some are downright benevolent. One is that of Tom Yawkey. A keeper of priceless barrier islands during his lifetime, he still walks beneath the moss-draped live oaks on the islands he so carefully preserved. His kindly and protective presence, reluctant to leave his island home, was perceived years ago by a young girl who knew him well and was glad his genial nature was still on the premises.

Blessed during his lifetime with the financial ability to help others, Yawkey in turn endowed the people of Georgetown County with a gift that will become more precious with every generation. Foreseeing the rampant development of every available South Carolina barrier island, he made sure that Georgetown County would always have two sea islands that remain unknown to many and wild to all.

Travelers far and wide are familiar with Georgetown

County's hauntingly beautiful Pawleys Island, the half-mile-wide, four-and-a-half-mile-long barrier island that lies between the county's mainland and the Atlantic Ocean. Only when travelers become more familiar with Georgetown does the realization dawn that the county has two other, larger barrier islands, North Island and South Island.

While Pawleys is open to the public via two causeways, the much larger South Island is accessible to only a few selected vehicles via the state's only government-operated ferry, which docks at neighboring Cat Island. Pawleys is covered with oceanfront and creek-front houses, but South Island has only the homes of a handful of permanent residents.

North Island, accessible only by boat, is resplendent with miles of wind-swept oceanfront and a working lighthouse nearly two centuries old. Boasting acres and acres of maritime forest and pristine marshland, the island is home to teeming wildlife but has no human residents. While many of the East Coast's fragile sand dunes are carefully monitored, fenced, renourished, and posted with warnings not to walk on and erode them, North Island's relatively untouched dunes average twenty to thirty feet. Two of the dunes reportedly measure fifty feet.

In this age of coastal population growth and development-related erosion, how have South and North islands remained pristine?

There is only one answer: the prudent, wise, and generous forethought of Tom Yawkey.

Born February 21, 1903, in Detroit, Michigan, Thomas Austin Yawkey became an orphan at a very early age. He was adopted by his uncle Bill—industrialist William H. Yawkey, owner of the Detroit Tigers baseball club.

One of three shareholders in the North and South island game preserves, William Yawkey eventually became sole owner. He came into the preserves in 1911 when he bought part of the property from the estate of the late Confederate brigadier general of artillery, Edward Porter Alexander, who had passed away in 1910. The general, legendary for his work in twelve major Civil War campaigns and battles, had purchased the North and South island plantation properties during the 1890s from struggling rice planters who had once prospered there. South Island's abandoned rice fields were teeming with ducks, and North Island, formerly the summer resort of many planters, was also a haven for waterfowl. Both islands had prolific populations of deer. At the turn of the twentieth century, General Alexander frequently hosted hunting parties for Northern acquaintances, most notably former president Grover Cleveland.

William Yawkey carried on this hunting tradition, instilling in his young nephew Tom the joys of outdoor life on the Low Country barrier islands. When William died at age forty-three in 1919, Tom, age sixteen, became a millionaire as well as owner of the properties collectively known as South Island Plantation.

The Yawkey holding now known as Cat Island, a portion of which was—and still is—privately owned, was then part of the mainland. When the Intracoastal Waterway was dug through Georgetown County in the 1920s, it cut Cat Island residents off from the mainland. The residents were given the choice of a bridge or a ferry. They chose the bridge. When that wooden bridge burned down later, the government constructed a ferry to replace it. The early ferry, which docked on either side of the waterway—or "government cut," as many still refer to it—ran via a steel cable that rose several feet out of the water when the ferry was in service. After the cable caused several serious accidents—at least one of them fatal—to boaters unfamiliar with the area, the ferry was changed so that the cable stayed under the water at all times.

The ferry was how Tom Yawkey and his guests accessed South Island. After alighting from the ferry onto Cat Island, they would travel through its forests until they reached the marshes and creek bridged by an earthen causeway leading to South Island, where Yawkey had his home.

In 1933, Tom, also in the tradition of his uncle, became a baseball team owner. He purchased the Boston Red Sox and was soon entertaining players at his barrier-island hunting enclave. Always alert to current events, the *Georgetown Times* immediately reported the visit of Ty Cobb to Yawkey's island home. It related the excellent shooting prowess of Cobb and most baseball players to their keen ability in tracking a baseball.

Yawkey built a large house facing North Island. Its placement was carefully selected for the breathtaking view of the North Island Lighthouse. The house was planned mostly by his wife, but Yawkey and she divorced before it was ready for her to take up residence. When Yawkey remarried, his new wife, Jean, declined to live in the spacious waterfront home her predecessor had designed. Instead, she and Yawkey resided happily and permanently in a prefabricated residence—a mobile home—that Yawkey shipped to the island.

During the late 1930s, he began managing his island properties as a waterfowl reserve. By experimenting with and adding to the early trunk-and-dike construction of General Alexander and the rice planters before him, Yawkey created more marshes, ones that could be controlled for water level and salinity level.

In 1966, he turned over the major management of the islands to his staff of wildlife biologists. Over the following decade, he supported and nurtured the evolution of waterfowl management for the properties. At the time of his death, he was no doubt pleased that his holdings of South Island, North Island, and part of Cat Island were well suited to the future. His will left the properties to the South Carolina

Wildlife and Marine Resources Department.

Four years prior to his death, Yawkey had become a benefactor to boys who needed homes or were not able to remain in their own homes. In 1972, his wife, Jean, had convinced him to buy land outside Georgetown near the Black River as a location for Tara Hall. More than three decades later, Tara Hall, which has its own school, is still a residential home for boys. Before her death, Jean began the tradition of sending the Tara Hall boys to an Atlanta Braves baseball game. She arranged for the Yawkey Foundation to continue that legacy.

Tom Yawkey died July 9, 1976. His legacy in Georgetown County lives on in the coastal islands that he nurtured. Thanks to his wisdom and foresight, anyone can experience what he did for Georgetown County in saving South Island, North Island, and a portion of Cat Island from the uncertainty of development. Though the Tom Yawkey Wildlife Center is open to education-minded visitors, one cannot simply drop in. The tour of Cat Island and South Island, limited to a maximum of fourteen visitors per week, must be booked long in advance. Visitors and residents still, as in Yawkey's day, reach the island via the ferry.

The tour is free of charge, yet priceless. From the moment each fortunate visitor walks onto the South Island ferry—which still docks at Cat Island—to the time, hours later, when he or she is returned to the dock for the ferry ride back to the mainland, wonders abound. Rare views of waterfowl, alligators, eagle nests, and coastline and marsh abound. The incredible scenery is matched by an equally wonderful historic and scientific narration by the center's resident wildlife biologist, Robert Joyner, who drives the tour vehicle.

For a true appreciation of the legacy left by Tom Yawkey, enjoy the tour. Then drive back to Georgetown and take a boat ride out to North Island. Walk past the jetty and keep going until all you can see to the north and the south are wide, pristine beaches without another soul around—except for maybe that of Tom Yawkey.

Alma Owens grew up on South Island, where her father was manager of Yawkey's island properties. She lived with her parents in a house surrounded by moss-draped live oak trees. The long gray tendrils of Spanish moss that grew from the trees' low-hanging branches swayed in the breeze and blew whenever storm-whipped winds hit the island.

"Mr. Yawkey and my daddy would always have coffee at five-thirty in the morning at our house," she recalled. "Daddy always had the coffee ready, because Mr. Yawkey would walk right on in.

"About a year after Mr. Yawkey died, I woke up at three o'clock in the morning. I heard the screen door shut. I got up, and Mama and Daddy were asleep, and nobody else was in the house. I looked out, and one of the porch rockers was just a-rockin'. I thought, 'Well there must be a big wind.' "

But then Alma looked outside. The Spanish moss hanging from the live oak trees was not moving even a breath. She knew then that there was no wind to rock the chair.

Even though no one she could see was present, she knew who had shut that screen door. It was Mr. Yawkey. Even the grave could not keep him from his beloved island.

Mr. Yawkey was still coming to visit.

Hopsewee

A solitary figure clothed in the colonial style affected by men in the 1770s has been seen walking down a lonely dirt road near the North Santee River on land formerly part of the vast Hopsewee Plantation. Carrying a lantern, the mysterious man heads toward Hopsewee's main house, the old home of Thomas Lynch II. Before he reaches the house, he disappears into thin air.

Is Thomas Lynch II, through his legendary strength of will, transcending time and the grave to come home to his beloved rivers?

The North and South Santee rivers flow eastward past the former rice fields of eighteenth- and nineteenth-century plantations. Just below Hopsewee, the two merge to form the wide and breathtaking Santee Delta. Beyond the delta, the rivers separate to meet the Atlantic.

Three generations of Lynches—Thomas Lynch, son Thomas Lynch II, and grandson Thomas Lynch III—nurtured

Hopsewee and its fertile lands. Thomas Lynch established Hopsewee. Thomas Lynch III, a signer of the Declaration of Independence, was born there. But it is Thomas Lynch II who haunts the plantation.

Thomas Lynch II loved the North and South Santee rivers. As a child, he understood that the tides of the rivers nourished the vast rice fields of his family's seven plantations. As an adult, he built his home and raised his family beside the flowing waters.

He frequently traveled away from his beloved rivers but always came back—until the last time he left.

Born in 1726, Thomas Lynch II presumed that should death befall him away from home, his remains would be brought back for a peaceful burial close to the rivers. That seemed a feasible request, for he was not only the patriarch of the second-wealthiest family in the state but a respected leader in the colonial government as well. He had every reason to feel confident that his well-known desire would be carried out.

But that was not to be. As a result of circumstance, Lynch died in Annapolis, Maryland, and was buried there, far from his beloved North and South Santee.

After two centuries, is he still seeking to make his way home?

The first Thomas Lynch began building Hopsewee in the late 1730s on a high bluff overlooking the North Santee River. From that commanding view, he could look out across the dark river to his rice fields on the other side. He died in 1738. In 1740, the house was completed according to his plans.

The North Santee was the lifeblood of Hopsewee and the main method of transportation to and from the plantation. Accordingly, the front of the house was built facing the river to receive guests who arrived by boat. Wide halls both upstairs and down opened from the front entrance to welcome the water-cooled breezes that blew off the river.

The great logs that could be seen floating down the river were the same kind of wood used in Hopsewee's construction—black cypress. Nearly impervious to both dampness and termites, black cypress gave Hopsewee the strength it needed to last for centuries. Also helping to preserve Hopsewee was its clapboard siding with a beaded edge. A hand-drawn bead, or channel, was cut just above the bottom edge of every cypress plank, which served to channel even the most torrential rains, rather than letting the water sink into the wood.

The great arches in the tall brick foundation were a feature of Hopsewee's airy, cool, ventilated cellar. The cellar allowed fresh air to circulate and kept the first floor—an entire story above the bricks laid in the damp earth—dry and fresh. The cellar's rear entrance allowed food to be brought in from the two kitchen buildings behind the house. Food was carried up the stairs from the cellar to the first-floor pantry before being served in the dining room. Like the parlor, Hopsewee's dining room faced the river.

The second floor consisted of four bedrooms. Like several rooms on the first floor, most of the bedrooms had hand-carved dentil molding around the ceilings and along the mantels over the fireplaces. Two rooms were adorned instead with more highly detailed candlelight molding, hand-carved in the form of lighted candles. Those two rooms—the formal parlor and the master bedroom of Thomas Lynch II above it—occupied the southeast corner of the house. A tall, high-ceilinged, dormered attic topped by twin chimneys and cypress shingles crowned Hopsewee.

For years, this was the house Thomas Lynch II came home to. Of all the acreage on the seven plantations his father had owned, the bluff where Hopsewee stood was his favorite.

Like his father before him, Thomas Lynch II made his son his namesake. After daughter Sabina was born in 1747 and daughter Esther in 1748, Thomas Lynch III was born to Thomas Lynch II and his wife, Elizabeth Allston, in 1749.

In 1751, Thomas Lynch II was elected to the colony of South Carolina's Commons House of Assembly as a delegate from the Parish of Prince George, Winyah. A dedicated public servant, he served in that capacity for over two decades.

By 1755, Elizabeth Allston had died and Thomas Lynch II had married again. His second wife was Hannah Motte. They soon had a daughter named Elizabeth.

Thomas Lynch II planted indigo as well as rice. A deep blue dye was derived from the root of the indigo plant. The dye was used to color the uniforms of the most powerful naval force in the world, the British navy. At that time, indigo was an even more lucrative crop than rice, so in 1755 Thomas Lynch II founded the Winyah Indigo Society and became its first president. Dues were paid in, of course, indigo.

In 1762, Lynch sold Hopsewee and moved to his other beloved Santee River. His new home was Peachtree Plantation on the South Santee.

By then, Lynch was a fiercely dedicated Patriot. He served on the Stamp Act Congress of 1765. In 1775, he was appointed as an adviser to General George Washington, along with co-advisers Benjamin Franklin and Colonel Benjamin Harrison. In that year, he also was elected to the First Continental Congress in Philadelphia.

In 1776, Lynch was scheduled to attend the Second Continental Congress, at which the Declaration of Independence was destined to be signed. Then tragedy struck. That February while in Philadelphia, he was paralyzed by a cerebral hemorrhage.

Thomas Lynch III, then twenty-six, was serving in the South Carolina militia. His request to leave and go to his ailing father was denied by his commanding officer, Christopher Gadsen. However, a higher calling overrode that denial. The Second Provincial Congress of South Carolina selected Thomas Lynch III as a delegate to join his father in Philadelphia at the Second Continental Congress. It was hoped that those two, the only father and son elected to the Continental Congress, would sign the Declaration of Independence together. Sadly, Thomas Lynch II was not able to do so. His son became the fifty-second and second-youngest signer of the historic document.

That December, while en route back to South Carolina, Thomas Lynch II died in Annapolis, Maryland. Though he had expected burial in South Carolina, an unknown grave in the churchyard of St. Anne's Episcopal Church in Annapolis became his final resting place.

Why was his request for home burial not carried out at the time of his death or soon afterward? And why was the grave of so great a Patriot not marked?

The answer may lie in the vast unrest that gripped the American colonies during the Revolutionary War. During those years, Lynch's remains stood a better chance of undisturbed interment in an anonymous grave far from his home. The graves of recently deceased Patriots were not always peaceful, as is illustrated in a shocking incident during which the remains of a great South Carolina Patriot were disinterred by British general Banastre Tarleton.

In this documented occurrence, the remains of Patriot brigadier general Richard Richardson were unceremoniously dug up six weeks after burial. The barbarous act was performed to torment his widow. The widow Richardson had been running the family plantation since the death of her husband and his interment in the plantation graveyard six weeks earlier. Her son Richard, who had been captured by the British in Charleston and incarcerated in prison camp, had been released after contracting smallpox. He went home to the Richardson plantation.

General Tarleton spread rumors he was leaving the area when, in fact, he was planning to ambush Patriot general Francis Marion, who was unaware that he was being stalked. The widow Richardson sent her son to tell Marion's men of Tarleton's impending attack.

Furious at having his plans thwarted, Tarleton commanded his men to dig up General Richardson from his grave, stating that he wanted to "look upon the face of so brave a man." That done, he demanded the Richardsons serve him dinner. After dinner, he had his men gather the Richardsons' livestock into the barn, where the corn harvest was stored. Then he ordered the barn burned to the ground. According to a report by General Marion, Tarleton beat the widow Richardson and left her with only the clothes she was wearing.

Obviously, the body of Thomas Lynch II, whose son signed the Declaration of Independence and who had been scheduled to sign it himself, was safer in an anonymous grave far from home while the war raged.

But why were his remains not brought back to his beloved home after the war?

He had a widow, three daughters, and a son. The person most likely to bring his remains home was Thomas Lynch III. However, Thomas Lynch III was in poor health. Nearly an invalid, he suffered from a "malingering" bilious illness he had contracted on a recruiting trip to North Carolina in 1775 during his tenure as a captain in the South Carolina militia. In 1779, he and his wife, the former Elizabeth Shubrick, set out for St. Eustatious in the West Indies in hopes of prolonging his life in a more favorable climate. Unfortunately, the voyage ended their earthly days. During a violent Caribbean storm, their ship was lost at sea with all aboard.

In his will, Thomas Lynch III requested that his father's

grave be moved to South Carolina. That request was never fulfilled.

Today, no one is sure exactly where in St. Anne's churchyard in Annapolis Thomas Lynch II is buried. Many of the early graves in St. Anne's had only wooden markers or are no longer marked by stones with legible inscriptions. And it is possible that Lynch's grave was purposely unmarked during the American Revolution for reasons of security. A great deal of the once-expansive burial ground of St. Anne's, established in 1692, lies on historic Church Circle. Now a paved streetscape with historic buildings, Church Circle was the property of St. Anne's and the site of many burials at the time of Lynch's death. In recent years, one grave was unearthed during roadwork. More than likely, Lynch's final resting place is now covered by a street or a building.

Wherever in or near St. Anne's churchyard his earthly remains lie, Lynch would rather they were interred, as he had requested, near his beloved Santee Rivers.

His old home, Hopsewee, has been much lived in and much loved. The house has been owned by only five families—the Lynches, the Hume-Lucases, the Wilkinsons, the Maynards, and the Beatties.

During the first two years they lived at Hopsewee, the Beatties hosted annual Revolutionary War reenactments. People portraying British military, American militia, and colonial civilians camped and cooked in authentic dress and manner under the live oak trees near the house. A battle between Tories and Patriots was reenacted behind the house. The Beatties, also in colonial dress, hosted tours of their home. A Sunday church service with attendees attired in period dress was held several miles away at the colonial-era Brick Church, where Thomas Lynch II, his family, and other St. James Santee Parish planters worshipped long ago.

The reenactments hosted by the Beatties were perhaps

the first time since the eighteenth century that the grounds at Hopsewee were filled night and day with people in colonial mode. All would-be Patriots and Tories behaved with enthusiasm and reverence for the period heralding the birth of the nation the Lynch family worked so diligently to help deliver. Thomas Lynch II and his family would no doubt have been very pleased.

One of the items that Raejean Beattie moved into Hopsewee was her grand piano. Soon afterward, while no one was downstairs, the piano was played—just a little. No doubt, someone was glad to have music at Hopsewee again!

Raejean related another experience: "About two years ago in June, Frank, my husband, was away on business and I was staying by myself. I was asleep and woke up to hear the voices of two Englishmen in conversation. They definitely had English—southern English—accents. I was definitely awake, and I certainly didn't want to meet them in the hall. I stayed in my room, turned on my radio, and went back to sleep."

Another British-related ghostly occurrence took place when portions of a movie were filmed at Hopsewee. The film portrayed the American Revolution from the British perspective. One part featured two female actors with Cockney accents running on the inside stairs. The women were filmed fully dressed in period clothing correct down to the corsets and other undergarments.

The women changed into and out of their Revolutionary War regalia in the Beatties' master bedroom—the same room where Thomas Lynch II once put on his own colonial shirts and breeches and where his first wife, Elizabeth Allston Lynch, no doubt donned her corset countless times. With little thought to the modesties of those who had lived at Hopsewee during the era being represented, the modern actresses had great fun parading immodestly around the room, lampooning the figure-enhancing corsets and flaunting their bosoms in shameless burlesque pantomime.

Later, when they were fully dressed in period costume, the actresses were photographed in the master bedroom. The movie was being made for national television, so no expense was spared for either equipment or film. When the pictures were developed, however, the film crew experienced an eerie surprise. Across the women's breasts and midsections—exactly where their corsets lay beneath their dresses—it looked as though a wind was whipping, blurring the portions of their bodies they had flaunted earlier. Except for those pictures, all other filming done at Hopsewee was perfect.

Two Tory women flaunting themselves immodestly in the master bedroom of a Patriot? No doubt, someone was displeased enough to ruin the photographs. Who could that someone be?

The lovely Elizabeth Allston Lynch, whose portrait hangs in the hall below?

Thomas Lynch III, who spent his early childhood in the home?

Or perhaps family patriarch Thomas Lynch II, comfortable in his former bedroom over the North Santee and asserting his authority still?

A family friend once stayed overnight at Hopsewee while the Beatties were out of town. He knew he was quite alone, yet during the night he heard the distinct sound of walking in the house.

"You know you have ghosts, don't you?" he said to the Beatties upon their return.

Mortal remains are earthbound, but spirits are not. Though the body of Thomas Lynch II was laid to rest far away, his immortal sense of *la vie dansante* and his love of home never strayed from his beloved Santee Rivers.

His spirit, free to roam, is surely home.

Kensington Park

Kensington Park was a magnificent dream that became a reality. During the Roaring Twenties—the days of Prohibition, flapper haircuts, and dancing the Charleston—Kensington Park was conceived just outside Georgetown. Offering a fabulous artesian swimming pool, a dance pavilion, and moonlight dining, the park provided two whirlwind summers of frolic before its halcyon days and nights came to a macabre musical end.

Well past the closing of the dance pavilion one sultry August night, Kensington Park ended in a mysterious fire. As the crackling flames reached their zenith, the electric player piano came to life as it burned, sending dance tunes jangling eerily into the night.

The cause of the blaze has never been discovered.

Kensington, on the Black River just outside Georgetown, was a prosperous rice plantation during antebellum days. In 1850, Kensington and Weehaw plantations, both owned by

Henry Augustus Middleton, together yielded nine hundred thousand pounds of rice. Little more than a decade later, the War Between the States began. Soon, the days of lucrative rice production ended.

Kensington's plantation house burned in the early 1920s. In the 1950s, the plantation, like a number of others near Georgetown, was developed into a residential area. For the past half-century, Kensington has been a thriving Georgetown neighborhood. The long entrance avenue to Kensington Plantation, now a residential street on the southern edge of the neighborhood, is perhaps the only trace left of the old plantation. No visible trace of Kensington's mid-1920s incarnation lingers. Nothing remains on the grounds today to attest that Kensington Park ever existed—but it did.

The owner of Kensington Plantation from 1908 through 1938 was J. Walter Doar. During that time, Kensington was still out in the country, though not many miles from the town limits.

In the early 1920s, the enterprising Mr. Doar began drilling deep into the fertile Kensington soil. Like many of our nation's entrepreneurial adventurers, he had an innovative strategy in mind. First, however, he needed a deepwater well. At a depth of seven hundred feet, he found the catalyst for his plan—a flowing, gushing, seemingly endless artesian well. Doar's discovery was the beginning of Kensington Park. He began designing a large cement swimming pool, to be fed by the flow from the artesian well.

Swimming—or "bathing"—in the ocean was very popular at nearby Pawleys Island. Visitors from all over the state rode the train to Georgetown County for just that purpose. Others preferred fresh water. Many county residents braved alligators, poisonous water snakes, dangerous drop-offs, and swift currents just to cool off in the coffee-hued waters of Georgetown's five rivers. How much more, reasoned Doar, would bathers enjoy swimming in the crystal-clear artesian-fed water of a safe cement pool?

In addition to the pool, Doar set aside other recreation areas within the park's fifteen acres. At tables under the ancient groves of live oaks, park visitors could hold afternoon picnics or elegant late-night formal dinners. As a *coup de grâce*, Doar built a dance pavilion.

In April 1924, the artesian pool was ready for bathers. Two hundred feet long and a hundred feet wide, it was a luxurious rarity. It had a shallow end two feet deep and a deep end of twelve feet. One hundred dressing rooms awaited eager bathers, as did a vast supply of towels and bathing suits for rent.

Kensington Park formally opened on April 22 with a grand ball—complete with Ellington's Symphony Orchestra—at the pavilion.

The artesian pool and the dance pavilion drew visitors from far and wide. The *Georgetown Times* began regularly mentioning the towns and counties from which visitors drove to cool off in Kensington's refreshing waters. Automobiles and trucks from Charleston, Manning, Sumter, Andrews, Hemingway, and Rhems regularly traveled to Georgetown bearing merry visitors.

Swimming in a cement pool fed by fresh artesian water was an exciting refreshment. And the dance pavilion proved nearly as popular. Numerous dances and parties were soon being held there. The regular Friday-night dance, usually serenaded by Ellington's Symphony Orchestra, was held all summer. Visitors could bathe all day, then dance the night away—if they wanted to get out of the pool, which was open at night, too.

A Halloween masked ball on October 31, 1924, did not herald the close of the park's first season. The pavilion was walled in and heaters were installed so dances could be held all winter long.

In the early summer of 1925, Kensington Park was well into its second successful season when a bill was introduced in the South Carolina legislature to prohibit public swimming pools. The bill was not passed. The *Georgetown Times* devoted little space to this silliness, offering only a brief, amused editorial comment questioning whether the instigator of the bill also planned to ban other waters, such as ponds and the ocean.

Kensington Park became a summer paradise. Chaperoned evening swim parties for young people were very popular. Nearly every delightful event at the park, from Sunday-school picnics to masquerade balls, was enthusiastically reported in the *Times*. Swimming and dancing parties, moonlight picnics, and late-night dinners abounded under the live oaks.

An "electric piano," or player piano, was installed in the pavilion so music for dancing would be available anytime the park was open. But not everyone enjoyed dancing. In fact, some folks felt dancing was downright evil, almost as wicked as males and females "bathing" together! And Kensington Park offered both those evils—dancing *and* "bathing"! Compounding this was a third evil—the illicit whiskey undoubtedly sneaked into the park by visitors.

There are no newspaper accounts of whiskey ever being consumed on the park's premises or anywhere else in Georgetown County at that time. After all, whiskey was illegal in the entire United States. The years Kensington Park existed—1924 and 1925—were during the height of Prohibition. However, the woods of Georgetown County were teeming with liquor stills. Rarely did a week pass that the *Georgetown Times* did not print an account of the most recent raids and seizures of local whiskey-making operations. Occasionally, if a still was particularly fancy, the Georgetown County sheriff and his deputies would display the contraption, complete with elaborately coiled copper tubes, in front of the town hall.

Beyond a doubt, whiskey making was a big illicit business in Georgetown County. Despite constant raids by law enforcement, liquor flowed nearly as freely as the five rivers did. Undoubtedly, whiskey concealed in hip flasks and handbags added to the merriment at Kensington Park.

On September 7, 1925, a scathing account of behavior at public swimming pools was put forth by Judge C. J. Ramage of Saluda, as reported in a newspaper account datelined Spartanburg.

Public swimming pools, the judge declared, brought disgrace to communities where they existed and threatened the foundation of civilization! He asked in no uncertain terms for the local grand jury to restrict the use of public swimming pools on the grounds that they led to a breakdown in morals. Residents, he stated, drove long distances—as far as thirty miles—to visit public pools "for purposes other than the pleasure of a swim." Married men who regularly visited pools, he said, favored spending time there with young unmarried women. Married women, he went on, came to the pools to spend time with unmarried men *and* boys. People were spending time at public pools not for swimming but for nefarious purposes. It was no wonder, he went on, that a drought had plagued South Carolina for allowing public pools to exist!

"The man who introduced a bill in the South Carolina Legislature to prohibit the public swimming pool was working along proper lines," finished Judge Ramage.

An account of the judge's declaration was printed in the *Georgetown Times* on September 11. The next issue of the *Times*, printed on September 18, carried shocking news. Sometime late Tuesday night, after the finish of the night's dance at 2:30 A.M., Kensington Park's pavilion had burned to the ground. Though the cause of the blaze was not known, "a cigarette carelessly dropped in some nook or corner, by someone of the dance crowd a short time before," was suggested as a likely answer.

Doar, the article added, carried very little insurance on the pavilion. He had lost a lucrative business and would not receive compensation. Obviously, he was not to blame. But who was?

What the article did not add was that the pavilion had burned just days after Judge Ramage's provocative accusations against public pools were printed in the *Georgetown Times*. Had someone, inflamed with moral anger by the allegations, deliberately set fire to the pavilion?

The next summer, Kensington Park's artesian pool opened once more. That season, however, lacked the carefree abandon of the first two. Of course, there was no dance pavilion. Music at one 1926 pool party was furnished, according to the *Times*, by "a small Victrola." The days of moonlight frolics from pool to pavilion had ended.

The burning of the pavilion, said Georgetown attorney Bill Doar, grandson of Kensington Park's J. Walter Doar, was one of a chain of events that led to his family's loss of the plantation in 1938.

Bill Doar has included Kensington Plantation, his earliest home, in one of his books, *Roofs Over My Head*. Born in 1935, he lived at Kensington Plantation until close to his third birthday. He grew up hearing family accounts of the plantation, the park, the artesian pool, the pavilion, and the fire. The fire, he said, had an eerie aspect.

"When the place was blazing," said Doar, "the player piano began playing."

Amid the smoke and flames, the strains of dance music rose into the summer night as the electric piano eerily played its last tunes.

The artesian pool, Doar added, was never destroyed. It was filled with dirt, and then trees were planted there. The remains of the pavilion, he said, were most likely used in housing built for the Civilian Conservation Corps workers stationed at the plantation some years later.

What caused the blaze that destroyed Kensington Park's pavilion and ended two years of legendary dancing and frolicking?

That question remains to be pondered late on sultry summer evenings, as does the mystery of the melody hauntingly loosed from the player piano on that long-ago night as the pavilion burned.

Pawleys Island Pavilion

Kensington Park's pavilion was not the only Georgetown County dance pavilion to burn to the ground mysteriously during the dark hours between midnight and dawn. One fateful June night in 1970, the most famous of the county's pavilions was consumed in an inferno that is believed to have been deliberately set. To this day, no one has been able to solve the mystery of what started—or who set—the fire that destroyed the last Pawleys Island Pavilion.

Chartered in 1960, the Pawleys Island Pavilion Company still exists—as if the pavilion might one day rise Phoenix-like from the spot near the ocean that has remained vacant ever since the last pavilion burned.

Every year as spring blossoms into summer, many an individual reminisces about the Pawleys Island Pavilion. Depending on the person, the memories are mostly fond and may focus on the last pavilion, the Old (Lafayette) Pavilion, the second pavilion, or the first pavilion. All four of the pavilions were physically on the island, not merely within Pawleys Island's mainland perimeter.

As early as 1920, a pavilion stood in the dunes on the Pawleys oceanfront just north of the south causeway. Molly Mercer's mother danced there as a twelve-year-old.

"They would get Mama and my future godfather, who was also about twelve years old, to start dancing when nobody else was," Mercer remembered. "Then the grownups would see these two children dancing, and they would start."

The first pavilion disappeared in the early 1920s.

Around 1925, the second pavilion was established near the middle of the island, close to the oceanfront sand dunes. Revelers of the mid- to late 1920s paid a quarter apiece for an evening of dancing to music played on the pavilion's Victrola. For those who reveled too heavily and chose not to drive home after the evening's festivities, a second-story loft afforded sleeping space.

"It was right out on the dunes in the middle of the island," said the late captain Sammy Crayton, who spent many pleasurable hours during the 1930s at the second pavilion. "There was a big, wide porch that opened right onto the beach on the prettiest spot on the island. The pavilion was lit up with lanterns. They didn't have lights on Pawleys Island then. Everything was lit up with lanterns or gas lights."

The second pavilion had a dance floor lined with seating. An upright piano, covered with a tarp against the dampness when not being played, was a fixture there. Cato and His Red Hot Peppers, a black band, played there most weekends. Cato was the piano player.

"We danced mostly the waltz and the foxtrot," said Captain Sammy. "We all took off our shoes and danced barefoot."

The second pavilion was open year-round, said the captain. Live entertainment arrived on weekends.

"The orchestra came over Saturday morning to prepare for Saturday night, and the dampness would have the piano keys stuck together. We'd fire up a couple of lanterns under a tarp in the morning so the piano would be ready for the piano player that night."

Captain Sammy recalled how cheap it was for a fellow to take a date to the second pavilion.

"It didn't cost you anything to dance," he said, "and all you had to buy was pop."

Soda pop was the only beverage officially sold at the second pavilion. Unofficially, though, corn whiskey could be had for a price.

"You could order it," said Captain Sammy, "and they came and buried it in the sand. You could buy a quart of corn liquor for seventy-five cents and a pint for fifty cents."

Other bands that appeared at the pavilion included the Clemson Jungle Aires and a Georgetown swing band, Belo Jones and His Five Men from Harlem. Surrounded by a soda bar and booths, the hardwood dance floor was home to the Big Apple and Little Apple dances.

It is not certain what became of the second pavilion. It closed around 1935 and is sometimes mistaken—by those who were born after its heyday—for its contemporary, a nightspot called The Towers. Built nearby on the mainland creek, The Towers purportedly was a wild place that burned to the ground after the owners had a falling out. One owner allegedly poured lacquer thinner throughout The Towers' attic and was blown out the end of the building by the blast that erupted when he ignited the solvent. Although The Towers was not a pavilion, it operated concurrently with the second of the pavilions. The alleged cause of The Towers' demise may have given rise to rumors years later, when the third and later the fourth pavilion also burned mysteriously.

The third pavilion, known as the Lafayette Pavilion or

the Old Pavilion, was built during the Great Depression. The Old Pavilion was a bare wood building on stilts located on the marsh on the west side of the south causeway. It stood across from the Sea View Inn.

Featuring shuttered windows for ventilation and marsh-directed plumbing, the Old Pavilion rang through the summer nights with the sounds of early shag music as teenagers and college students perfected their versions of what would become the most famous dance in the state of South Carolina.

Doc Baldwin remembered three generations of the same families spending time there.

"Everyone had a good time," Baldwin said. "That was the last pavilion I remember as a family place. Of course, you'd have the local folks and tourists there, and things tended to get a little touchy sometimes. I remember fights in there, especially when there were house parties."

The Old Pavilion burned down, circumstances unknown, in 1957. Although rumors of foul play circulated, old wiring was finally blamed for the fire.

The New Pavilion was, for the most part, the 1960 project of Old Pavilion alumni who wanted the same youthful island experiences for their progeny. It was also intended to keep fun-loving young people close to home.

The Pawleys Island Pavilion Company was chartered in 1960 with a president, a secretary-treasurer, a board of directors, and nearly fifty members. To belong to the company, each member paid $100 and promised to loan, if necessary, as much as $750 to the New Pavilion cause. The purpose of the company was not to make money, but rather to benefit island young people by providing entertainment. One bylaw of the company said, in effect, that if the corporation were dissolved, a Georgetown County charity would receive its assets.

With the help of State Senator James Morrison of Georgetown, a road was built southeast from the beach road to the causeway. There, on stilts in the creek, the new wooden pavilion rose. It had generous porches and proper modern indoor restrooms.

For ten years, the New Pavilion was a living legend complete with live music. Otis Goodwin and the Castanets, the Travelers, Maurice Williams and the Zodiacs, Drink Smalls, the Jetty Jumpers, the Rivieras, the Monzas, the Sensational Epics, Harry Parker and the Caravelles, the Embers, the Catalinas, and other bands entertained on summer weekends. The joint was jumping!

Barry McCall was a bartender at the New Pavilion for three years.

"The Travelers was probably the hottest band we had play there," said McCall, who no longer stands behind the bar but sits on the bench—as Pawleys Island magistrate. "Everybody who worked there was involved in booking the bands. A lot of the very prominent people in music were just starting out. We would bring them down and give them a place to stay—and that was about all the pay they got."

Maurice Williams and the Zodiacs played the New Pavilion three separate weekends the summer their song "Stay" became a hit, he noted.

McCall remembered the pavilion as a place for everyone.

"It's hard to relate in words," he said, reflecting on the atmosphere of the island's gathering place. "There were groups from eight- or nine-year-olds to eighty- to ninety-year-olds. We had very little underage drinking; we carded everybody. I got a lot of tips from eighty- to ninety-year-old people that I'd carded!

"From the time we'd open during the day in the summer to the time we closed the doors at night, we'd have a low average of two hundred people during the week to five hundred people on a summer weekend. Some were local; some came from Georgetown; some came from Andrews. Then there were the people staying on the island. You wouldn't have a family of two or three renting a house like you do now. There'd be ten or fifteen, and they'd all come to the pavilion. They'd bring babies. It was a family beach and a family pavilion.

"Once in a while, we'd have a fight, but never a heavy one," said McCall. "We had a deputy, Claude Altman, and he had a sub-deputy, Wolfe—a big dog."

Altman was the only deputy on Pawleys Island then, remembered Doc Baldwin.

"Wolfe was a German police dog—and he was the crowd control. You didn't have knifings and shootings like you do now."

Having grown up going to the Old Pavilion, Baldwin did not spend much time at the new one, but he remembered it as being more lively than its predecessor.

"I went in the service in '59 and never went in that one much," Baldwin said. "It was more of a jam-packed, hard-rockin', hard-drinking kind of place."

On June 16, 1970, fire claimed the New Pavilion. The June 18 issue of the *Georgetown Times* had a picture of the smoking ruins on the front page.

"The Pawleys Pavilion, enjoyed by young people for a decade, burned to a total loss about 5 A.M. Tuesday with only the piling remaining," the paper noted. "Flames had engulfed the building when the fire was detected and the alarm sounded by a nearby resident, Larry Holliday. . . . The cause of the fire is unknown."

"I had just finished school in Atlanta," said Barry McCall, "and my wife and I were living on the island. I saw the big orange glow in the sky and just sat on the edge of the bed and cried."

But what caused the fire?

"Anytime you have a fire like that, there's always a rumor," McCall said. "There was a lot of rumor, and a lot of mourning."

No explanation could be found that the fire was accidental. The general consensus was that arson caused it, though most folks did not know who or why. And those who knew were not saying.

Rumors persist to this day that it was arson—that someone paid someone else a hundred dollars to do it. The someone who set the fire, according to the rumor, is dead now, but the someone who paid that person is not. As for motive, a grudge has been rumored for years—someone who was thrown out of the pavilion sought revenge by having it burned down so no one else could enjoy it.

To date, a fifth pavilion has never come about, although the Pawleys Island Pavilion Company is still in existence.

"People ask me," said Molly Mercer, whose grandfather was a member of the company, "if there's going to be another one built, and I say, 'Well, if it hasn't been built yet, it's probably not going to be.' "

A short distance from the ocean, the triangle of land where the last pavilion stood is now a grassy space, the reminder of a legend that went up in smoke decades ago, gone like the dance music that used to drift across the marsh on summer evenings.

It is on that triangle that the Pawleys Pavilion Reunion is held each spring. For one magical May evening, the spirit of the last pavilion is revived, with many of the habitués of the vanished pavilion in attendance.

"I've been asked many times why we have it there," Molly Mercer said, "and I just tell them, 'We have to have it where the ghosts are.' "

Fiddler's Green

The Georgetown County coast abounds with seafaring tales and mysteries, from colonial pirate stories right up to present-day adventures. Among the latter is the saga of the ill-fated schooner *Fiddler's Green*.

The twin Crayton brothers were born in 1915. Christened Richard and Samuel, Dickie and Sammy grew up loving boats and the sea. Georgetown County, with its busy international seaport, wind-swept barrier islands, and five winding rivers, was the base for their countless maritime adventures.

When the hurricane of 1916 approached Georgetown County, the young brothers and their mother were on Pawleys Island at the seaside boardinghouse she ran there. A man driving a horse-drawn buckboard stopped at the boardinghouse and told Mrs. Crayton that, but for him, she and her baby boys were the last people on the narrow barrier island. Due to all the last-minute work of preparing the boardinghouse for the storm, Mrs. Crayton had not realized that everyone else was gone. Since no other transportation was available, she loaded her twin sons on the man's buckboard and left Pawleys Island for the mainland. They crossed the narrow bridge linking the sections of earthen causeway just in time. Shortly after their passage, the causeway was washed away as the hurricane ravaged the island.

This early incident set the tone for Dickie and Sammy's adventures, including that of the *Fiddler's Green*.

The legend of Fiddler's Green is an ancient one. It tells how an old sailor ready to leave the sea can find utopia on land. He should begin walking inland carrying an oar on his shoulder, finally traveling far enough that the locals have never seen boats, oars, or the ocean. When he comes upon a lovely township in the heart of a beautiful countryside and someone looks curiously at his oar and asks what he is carrying, he will know he has arrived in Fiddler's Green. There, he will be given his own seat beside the village inn. His pipe will always be filled with fragrant tobacco, and his glass of ale will magically fill up anytime he drinks the last drop. He will savor his ale and pipe while watching village maidens dance to fiddle music on the village green before the inn.

Fiddler's Green, the sailors' legendary destination after leaving the sea, was the perfect name for a vessel that came out of the sea to rest high and dry on the south end of Pawleys Island.

Friday, January 23, 1953

Fiddler's Green was a fifty-foot wooden-hulled schooner. Made almost entirely of red Honduran mahogany, she was as beautiful a craft as ever plied the Atlantic. Launched in 1937, she was well seasoned, widely traveled, and outfitted with a new diesel engine by the time this story took place.

The schooner belonged to a Maryland physician, Edmund B. Kelly of Baltimore. Dr. Kelly and three companions were taking her down the East Coast before heading farther south. Their destination was the island of Trinidad, eleven miles off the coast of Venezuela in the southern Caribbean.

Little did Dr. Kelly and his crew realize that this would be the last journey for *Fiddler's Green*. They had no way of knowing the schooner would never reach Trinidad.

Most of the first leg of the journey involved sailing or motoring down the Intracoastal Waterway. On that fateful January night in 1953, however, *Fiddler's Green* was motoring down the South Carolina coast in the unpredictable Atlantic rather than the sheltered inland waterway. Her engine was running because the night was too calm for her sails to be of any use. With the moon in its first quarter, visibility was moderate.

The night passage along the four-and-a-half-mile Pawleys Island shore should have been uneventful. *Fiddler's Green* would have passed the island without ever breaching the shore had it not been for one catastrophic oversight.

During their passage south, the four-member crew of *Fiddler's Green* took turns with the responsibility of four-hour night watches while the others slept. On that fateful night, the watch changed as the schooner cut through the dark Atlantic off Pawleys. The crew member whose watch was ending unthinkingly left a metal flashlight near the compass just before he relinquished the helm to the next watch. The crew member whose watch was beginning did not notice the flashlight. If he had, he would have realized that the metal object had immediately caused a serious deviation in the compass reading. As he carefully piloted *Fiddler's Green* according to the compass, he had no idea he was steering her closer and closer to Pawleys Island.

Had the night been windy enough for sailing, the sound of breakers crashing on the island might have warned him of the dangerous proximity of the beach. Instead, the powerful diesel engine obliterated the sound of the waves.

Minutes later, there came a low grinding sound as the long, graceful keel plowed deeply into the golden sand. *Fiddler's Green* had run aground on the south end of Pawleys Island.

The tide was higher than usual that night, and *Fiddler's Green* sailed onto sand that was rarely submerged. When her keel plowed into the bottom, the schooner still had a chance to get back to sea. But that opportunity was lost when everyone aboard woke up and another well-meaning crew member tossed the anchor onto the highest part of the south end. As the tide went out, the anchor held fast and the keel nestled deeper and more firmly into the hard-packed sand.

When morning dawned, the tide had gone out, leaving the twenty-eight-ton schooner beached far from the water on the highest part of the south end of Pawleys. It might be months, even seasons, before the tide rose that high again. And accessibility was not good. Far beyond the sand lay Pawleys Creek to the east, the south-end swash to the south, the Atlantic to the east, and a distant parking lot to the north.

The tug *Robert W.* and the Coast Guard cutter *Travis* motored up from Georgetown Harbor to assist *Fiddler's Green*. Neither vessel was able to rescue the beached schooner. Sand had washed in around her keel, holding her fast. Crew members from the tug and the cutter were quoted in the *Georgetown Times* as saying the schooner's keel "was set in concrete."

Dr. Kelly's insurance company hired Captain Harry V. Salmons of Salmons Co., Marine Contractors, to salvage *Fiddler's Green*. Unwilling to accept the schooner after the estimated costs of refloating, dry-docking, and major repairs, Dr. Kelly accepted fifteen thousand dollars from his insurance company and abandoned the vessel. Too far from the water, her long, graceful keel wedged deeply in the sand, the thirty-thousand-dollar schooner was sold by the insurance company for less than five thousand dollars.

Dickie and Sammy Crayton were by now seasoned mariners with the hard-earned title of *captain* before their names. Along with Beverly Sawyer and William F. Rutland, they purchased *Fiddler's Green* from the insurance company and began the daunting task of getting her back to sea in one piece before sailing her down to her new home in Georgetown Harbor.

No one doubted that the brothers could save *Fiddler's Green*, even though the insurance company had given up. Dickie and Sammy knew the owners, captains, and crews of every tugboat and shrimp trawler in Georgetown County. Within that vast array of men and boats were more than enough manpower, horsepower, experience, skill, and knowledge to float nearly any vessel that had the misfortune to go aground. They just had to wait until the conditions were right.

Dickie and Sammy were ready for the challenge. They were also patient. They knew that floating the schooner would require a precise tide, wind direction, and phase of the moon. *Fiddler's Green* was theirs. After she was unearthed from her sandy hold and repaired, she was going to sea again.

In the meantime, guarding *Fiddler's Green* was an ongoing task. In order to prevent would-be salvagers from dismantling and pillaging the schooner, she had to be manned at all times. If she was left alone, miscreants could remove her delicate gauges, brass cleats, pulleys, hundreds of yards of line, sails—the list was endless. Thieves could break the glass in her hatches, climb aboard, and steal to their hearts' content. The schooner's dinghy alone—a four-man vessel of solid mahogany—was a prize.

Dickie and Sammy made sure they or someone they trusted was with *Fiddler's Green* at all times. They spent those many hours painstakingly repairing some of the damage that had occurred when the schooner grounded.

After over a month of guarding *Fiddler's Green* around the clock, the eve of her floating finally arrived. The following morning promised a higher-than-usual lunar high tide, a strong west wind, and clear skies. Powerful tugboats and commercial shrimp trawlers from Georgetown were scheduled to arrive the next morning to pull the schooner back into the Atlantic.

Their vigil nearly over, Dickie and Sammy were in high spirits, ready to get *Fiddler's Green* to Georgetown. Only one more night of guarding her lay before them. Their companions had finished their watches and were not scheduled to return until morning for the refloating. In the day's excitement, Dickie and Sammy had not made any arrangements for supper. Now, they were ravenous.

Since the moment they had claimed *Fiddler's Green*, she had not been left for even a short time without someone watching her. Surely, they reasoned, it would be safe to depart for half an hour so both of them could take a break and drive into Georgetown for a bite to eat. The Whistling Pig, located on the Pawleys Island side of Georgetown, was only fifteen minutes away. The Pig made the best and fastest hamburgers around. The temptation was unbearable—fifteen minutes there and fifteen minutes back for a delicious, mouth-watering hamburger. Surely, it would be all right to leave the schooner for less than an hour on this last day.

Their decision made, Dickie and Sammy walked across the sand a good half-mile to where their car was parked. Everyone, they reasoned, knew how closely the schooner had been guarded for the past weeks. No one would dare breach her resting place now. Besides, what could vandals do in such a short period? They would not have time to carry anything away. They would have to walk too far, and there was no cover, only open beach.

Thirty-five minutes later, Dickie and Sammy arrived back at their parking place near the south end. Having eaten their burgers on the way, they now looked forward to the walk back to the schooner. But as soon as they got out of the car, they knew something was not right. As they neared the vessel, a horrible sight came into focus.

Hanging from the tilted mast was a body!

Dickie and Sammy broke into a run. Who could have hanged himself on the vessel, and why?

When they reached *Fiddler's Green*, the sight was even more macabre up close. The body, silhouetted by the setting sun, swung slowly in the breeze. Wordlessly, the brothers cut the rope holding it.

When the form fell to the sand, Dickie and Sammy received an even bigger surprise. This was no body! Someone had stuffed one of the schooner's foul-weather outfits—boots, hood, and all—and suspended it from the mast.

One of their friends must have played a joke on them. The brothers immediately began to look for a note or evidence of the identity of who had pulled the prank.

They found not a single clue.

They did discover, however, that the schooner's fine dinghy was gone. No drag marks crossed the sand. The dinghy was very heavy. From all the recent activity, footprints were everywhere. Had someone—or several someones—carried the weighty dinghy to the distant parking lot? Or had they carried it to the ocean or the creek and rowed away?

Carrying did not seem feasible—the dinghy was just too

heavy. The incoming tide had covered up any telltale signs that might have been at the water's edge. Had someone been watching all the time, waiting for just the right moment? If so, how on earth had they found time to carry off the dinghy *and* prepare the dummy *and* haul it up in the air? It was not humanly possible.

Dickie and Sammy also found it was not humanly possible to float *Fiddler's Green* and sail her away. She was grounded too fast at too remote a location. They completed their salvaging by stripping *Fiddler's Green* right there on the beach at the south end of Pawleys Island.

Neither hide nor hair was ever seen of the missing mahogany dinghy. Its inexplicable disappearance and the eerie hanging of the foul-weather gear remain mysteries to this day.

Captain Dickie's Narrow Escape

One summer evening in the late 1930s, young Dickie Crayton received a phone call at his home in Georgetown from a young lady friend who needed a favor. Could Dickie drive her over to Pawleys Island? She had made plans to meet some other young ladies at the Pawleys Island Pavilion. Her friends were staying on the island, but she was in Georgetown and did not have a ride. Dickie agreed to drive her.

The pavilion at that time was built on stilts so that it stretched out over the salt marsh on the west side of the barrier island. A good time could nearly always be found there. Young people from Georgetown as well as those staying on the island thronged to the pavilion. Known for its dancing, live bands, and happy camaraderie, it was a popular meeting place.

Driving north out of Georgetown, Dickie and the young lady talked happily about mutual friends and acquaintances. They were glad to be able to drive to Pawleys without having to board the old automobile ferry. Crossing over the new two-lane bridge just outside Georgetown was much more convenient than waiting for the ferry. The bridge crossed the channel just below the point where it divided into the separate Black and Pee Dee rivers. Next, it crossed the narrow island separating the channel from the Waccamaw River, then headed across the wide Waccamaw. At last, the dark bridge ended. They drove onto the southern end of the Waccamaw Neck, the twenty-mile-long isthmus of fertile forest bordered by the Waccamaw River and its rice fields on the west and the Atlantic Ocean on the east. Nine miles north up the Waccamaw Neck on the Atlantic Ocean lay their destination, the four-and-a-half-mile-long Pawleys Island. Eleven miles north of the center of Pawleys, the Waccamaw Neck ended at the fishing village of Murrells Inlet on the northern edge of Georgetown County.

Now, at the end of the bridge and the beginning of the Waccamaw Neck, Dickie and his friend headed into the total darkness of the Low Country night, the blackness broken only by the twin beams of their headlamps. To the left, or west, lay Arcadia, the vast Vanderbilt-owned estate comprised of the antebellum rice plantations Prospect Hill, Forlorn Hope, Bannockburn, Oak Hill, Clifton, Rose Hill, George Hill, and Fairfield. Hobcaw Barony, the sprawling property of Bernard Baruch, lay east, to their right. Like Arcadia, Hobcaw Barony was made up of many former rice plantations. No lights shone from either Arcadia or Hobcaw Barony. Their grand plantation houses were far from the Kings Highway, deep among the moss-laden live oaks and towering pines. No lights shone on the narrow, two-lane Kings Highway either. But for the headlamps of their automobile, the darkness of the Waccamaw Neck was complete.

It was not unusual to drive from Georgetown to Pawleys Island or even the entire length of the Waccamaw Neck without meeting even one other vehicle.

All of a sudden, the light of a single headlamp appeared in the darkness coming around a distant bend. They would soon, it appeared, meet a motorcycle. The single light grew closer and closer, and they could hear the faint guttural sound of the only vehicle they were likely to pass on their lonely trek. The headlamp kept coming, the engine growing louder and louder, until the approaching vehicle was only seconds away.

Suddenly, a glowing white figure clothed in flowing folds of pale gossamer appeared in the air right in front of their automobile.

"It looked like a lady wearing a dress with a long train," Captain Dickie recalled. "She was up in the air, so the train didn't flow behind her. It hung straight down—right in front of the windshield on my side of the car."

Dickie swung the steering wheel to the right, barely missing the figure. At that instant, the vehicle with the single headlamp whizzed by on his left.

It was no motorcycle.

Inches from Dickie's face—exactly where his automobile would have been had he not swerved—an unlighted headlamp whooshed by. The vehicle they had thought was a motorcycle was in fact a motorcar with one lamp burned out.

Dickie and his friend were speechless in their shocked relief. What a narrow escape! Had the figure not appeared in the air in front of their vehicle, Dickie would never have swerved. They would have crashed head-on into the vehicle with the burned-out light.

Neither Dickie nor the young lady ever forgot their narrow escape.

Years later, married and living far from Georgetown, the once-young lady told her children, and later her grandchildren, of her and Dickie's adventure. Then, on a visit to Georgetown, she introduced her grandchildren to Captain Dickie.

"Remember that story I've been telling you all these years about the lady who appeared in the sky and saved my friend and me from wrecking? This man," she told them proudly, "is my friend Dickie. He was driving that night we saw the lady up in the air with her gown flowing down in front of the car—the lady who made us swerve around her to save ourselves."

Lost Treasure of the Confederacy

Could the remains of the lost Confederate treasury lie buried on a Georgetown rice plantation?

One of the South's most enduring and legendary mysteries is the disappearance of the Confederate States of America treasury. The well-guarded fortune including gold bars, silver, and jewelry was rushed out of Richmond, Virginia, by the Confederate government at the end of the Civil War under the auspices of Secretary of the Treasury George Alfred Trenholm just hours before the city was captured by Federal troops. In the confusion of the evacuation, President Jefferson Davis, Trenholm, and the rest of Davis's Cabinet lost control of events. During the chaos of their flight south, most of the treasury disappeared. Much of it was never found and remains unaccounted for to this day.

Did the Federal cavalry who finally captured President

Davis in Georgia plunder the treasury? Or was it divided during evacuation, never even reaching Georgia? Or had it already been spirited away by the greatest blockade runner of all time? Did handsome and dashing blockade runner *extraordinaire* George Alfred Trenholm secretly bury the fortune on one of his Georgetown rice plantations for safekeeping?

A daring but shrewd Charleston businessman, Trenholm was one of the most intriguing characters of the Civil War. He owned the Confederacy's premier blockade-running fleet and masterminded its strategy. In 1863, using the profits of his highly successful blockade running, he added five Georgetown County rice plantations to his impressive list of real-estate holdings. In 1864—the same year he became secretary of the Confederate treasury—he bought a sixth. After the war, he lost nearly all of his property but somehow managed to keep his Georgetown plantations. Could the lost treasury be buried on one of those landholdings?

The son of a Charleston shipper, Trenholm began working as an accountant for the Charleston shipping firm Fraser and Company in 1822 at age sixteen. Later, he became its clerk. Well versed in all aspects of maritime trade, he began writing articles against Northern tariff laws in 1830. In 1842, due to his determination to better connect Charleston with other parts of the country, the South Carolina Railroad elected him its director.

He was by 1853 senior partner and principal owner of both Fraser and Company and its British branch office, Fraser, Trenholm & Company, headquartered in Liverpool. Those two companies and Trenholm Brothers in New York specialized in importing and exporting. Well versed in the intricacies of government, Trenholm served in the South Carolina legislature from 1852 to 1856. In 1861, he was elected one of South Carolina's commissioners of defense. His diverse business skills led him to own interests in wharves, steamships, railroads, hotels, cotton presses, banks, and plantations.

Long before the Civil War, Fraser, Trenholm & Company was prepared for wartime import and export. Cotton grown in the South and shipped to Lancashire County, England, was necessary for the Lancashire cotton mills. During the year prior to the war, Fraser, Trenholm & Company began a five-ship line of trade between Charleston and Liverpool. His shipping connections thus firmly ensconced, Trenholm was braced for the inevitability of the War Between the States.

When South Carolina seceded from the United States on December 20, 1860, the port of Charleston was free to disregard the high import tariff charged by Northern ports. Other Southern states and their ports followed suit. The tariff remained nearly 50 percent in United States ports but was very low in the ports of the seceded Southern states.

Merchants in New York, Boston, and other Northern ports grew fearful that European markets would avoid them in favor of the lower tariffs in the South. President Abraham Lincoln told the Northern merchants that the United States would continue to levy an equal tariff on Southern ports. The Southern ports refused to comply because they were no longer United States ports, but rather Confederate States of America ports. Charleston officials declined to relinquish their customs house to United States officials. The Federal occupation of Fort Sumter at the entrance to Charleston Harbor and the blockade of the port prevented any importing and exporting. The Confederates fired a shot toward Fort Sumter from the Charleston waterfront, and the Civil War began. The newly formed Confederate government now had to arm, outfit, and finance a war against a nation nearly a century old.

The United States blockade of Southern ports was detrimental to not only the Confederacy but to Britain as well. While the South needed its ports open to export cotton to

Britain to fund war supplies, Britain needed the shipments of cotton to keep its Lancashire cotton mills running.

Confederate purchasing agents in Britain bought supplies for the newly formed Southern military. Many of the purchasing contracts were covered by Fraser, Trenholm & Company. For such services as procuring arms and artillery and purchasing uniforms and other military clothing for the Confederate stores, Fraser, Trenholm & Company received 10 percent.

In the meantime, Trenholm implemented a unique agreement with the Confederate government. Through this exclusive arrangement, his firm shipped Southern cotton to Liverpool. The cotton was then sold in Britain and the proceeds placed in British banks. With the profits, agents in Britain purchased provisions to support the war and shipped them to the Confederacy via Trenholm's blockade-running ships. Charles Prioleau, one of Fraser, Trenholm & Company's five directors—all of whom were South Carolinians—became a British citizen so he could legally export goods from England to ports in the South.

Fraser, Trenholm & Company was in effect the Confederacy's exclusive banker in Britain. In fact, James D. Bulloch, head financial agent of the Confederacy in Europe, had his office in the Liverpool branch of Fraser, Trenholm & Company. In 1861, for a commission of half a percent, Fraser, Trenholm & Company became a depository of the Confederate government, with half a million dollars in credit toward purchases for the Southern states.

As the war began, Trenholm foresaw a serious need for a Confederate navy. Not long after the capture of Fort Sumter, he found an opportunity for the South to purchase at half price a fleet of armed vessels, a ten-ship armada of first-class Indiamen from the British East India Company. This would have cost the South the equivalent of forty thousand of the three million dollars' worth of government cotton bales it was storing. Trenholm advised General P. G. T. Beauregard that the Confederacy would be wise to buy the steamships not only to build a navy but to help ship cotton to Britain. Beauregard took the plan to President Jefferson Davis, who declined. The South did not buy the vessels, leaving its coast vulnerable to Federal blockades and attacks.

Soon, the Confederacy was in desperate need of warships. Trenholm had strong connections with shipyards in England and Scotland, thanks to their having built a number of fast steamships for his blockade running. He arranged for those shipyards to construct vessels to naval-warship specifications but without armaments, per Britain's Foreign Enlistment Act, which allowed for the building but not the equipping of ships for foreign nations. Once each new sailing ship, complete with powerful steam engines, left British territorial waters, she was met by supply ships waiting to outfit her with battery, ammunition, and crew. Nassau was often the meeting place for the transformations. Although the United States government grew suspicious, then knowledgeable, of this activity, it was not able to prevent Trenholm from having ships built for the Confederate navy. The more suspicious Northern spies grew, the more closely guarded the precautions became.

Ships' names were changed, as were their ownerships, to cause confusion. Trenholm had the *Alabama*, for example, built during the height of Northern suspicion toward his British shipyard connections. The vessel was known during construction only as "Hull 290." Suspicion was so high that she was launched several days early. By the time British authorities came to seize her, she was long gone. Christened the *Enrico*, she left port on July 29, 1862, for a trial run with numerous dignitaries on board. Instead of bringing the ladies and gentlemen back to Liverpool after their dining cruise on the Mersey River, she transferred them to a smaller vessel, put to sea, and headed for the Azores, where she received ammunition and battery and was rechristened the CSS *Alabama*. Two weeks later, on August 13, Captain Raphael Semmes took charge of the newly outfitted ship. By June 1864, she had captured and burned fifty-five Federal merchantmen. She wreaked havoc upon the Federal cause until she was sunk off France that August.

Other shippers ran the Federal blockade during the war, but Fraser, Trenholm & Company was by far the largest and most successful. It often routed shipments to Nassau or Bermuda, to be forwarded to Confederate destinations. In order to mislead the Federal navy, shipping manifestos filled out in England stated Nassau or Bermuda as the final destination for cargoes. In reality, they were merely stopping-off ports for the precious shipments destined for Charleston (only 515 miles from Nassau and 772 miles from Bermuda), Wilmington (674 miles from Bermuda), or Savannah (834 miles from Bermuda). Large vessels registered in Britain would bring the shipments to Bermuda or Nassau. The smaller, swifter blockade runners would then take on the cargo and complete the deliveries to Southern ports.

Aware they were being watched by the Federal navy, blockade-running captains often used decoys to lure attention away from the vessels about to take on cargo from Britain and head for Confederate ports. One blockade runner, the *Cecile*, ran so close to the blockade that Northern shots knocked over cotton bales on her deck. Her chief engineer fueled the engine with coal dust, creating a dark smokescreen. The *Cecile* was then fed with clean fuel, ran right through the smoke-filled blockade, and disappeared.

Early in the war, Fraser, Trenholm & Company proved it was possible to legally run the blockade. They paid a cunning arms broker named Grazebrook to stockpile firearms disguised as pottery in his warehouse in England. Through change of consignment and shipment ownership that took place nearly faster than the necessary documents could be signed—too fast for a paper trail until it was too late— Trenholm and his associates arranged for one of their newly purchased two-thousand-ton steamers, the *Bermuda*, to make a run from Britain to Savannah and back.

The *Bermuda* loaded up in Liverpool with the firearms Grazebrook had procured, as well as other military supplies. Before United States consul F. H. Morse could blink an eye, the *Bermuda* had delivered to Savannah a grand cornucopia of aids for the war effort—precious medical supplies; 6,500 Enfield rifles with 200,000 cartridges; 22 cannons; cannon powder and shot; cannon carriages; 60,000 pairs of army shoes; 20,000 blankets; and 180 barrels of gunpowder. Not only was the delivery successfully made, but the *Bermuda* loaded up with a huge cargo of Georgia cotton before running the blockade again as she left Savannah for Liverpool.

Blockade running kept the war going. For example, in April 1862, on the Saturday evening before the battle at Shiloh, Tennessee, the blockade runner *Kate*, named after Trenholm's daughter-in-law, arrived at Charleston loaded with a thousand barrels of gunpowder and weaponry for ten thousand men. Beginning Sunday morning and lasting into the night, the shipment was loaded onto wagons, taken to the train depot, and sent to Shiloh. At the end of November 1862, the *Kate* was caught by the Federal navy—but only after running the blockade to enter Confederate ports forty-four times.

Trenholm's ship captains became legendary for their skill, daring, and tenacity. One of them, Scottish captain William Wilson, recaptured his ship from the Federal navy. Wilson was captain of the *Emily St. Pierre*. Not only was the ship named after Trenholm's daughter Emily St. Pierre Trenholm, a figurehead made in the young lady's likeness adorned the bow. When the *Emily St. Pierre* was captured while attempting to run the blockade into Charleston, Captain Wilson recaptured her with the aid of his cook and steward, the rest of his crew having been taken off the ship.

Blockade running had a high success rate. According to the *London Index*, 498 out of 590 attempts by steamships to run the blockade at Wilmington and Charleston between January 1863 and April 1864 were successful.

Trenholm's ships, when unable to get past the blockade of Charleston Harbor, came into the port of Georgetown before Georgetown Harbor was blockaded.

One of Trenholm's blockade runners, the *Nashville*, had been a Southern naval vessel—the first warship to fly the Confederate banner in British territorial waters. After capturing sixty-six thousand dollars' worth of Federal prizes, she was sold to Trenholm for use as a blockade runner. The *Nashville* was received in Georgetown unbeknownst to Federal officials, who did not realize Georgetown was not blockaded. There, she had all her armaments removed and was renamed the *Thomas L. Wragg*. She then left Georgetown without the Northern officials who were searching for her ever knowing she had been in port. She soon delivered sixty thousand rifles and forty tons of powder to Wilmington and carried away an entire load of cotton. She arrived in Bermuda sometime later after being chased from Charleston by four blockading ships, one of which pursued her for four hours.

After Georgetown was blockaded in 1862, Trenholm's runners continued to access its port.

Every run by Fraser, Trenholm & Company was not successful. Several of Trenholm's ships were wrecked while attempting to run the blockade into Charleston Harbor. One was the 226-foot *Georgiana*, named for a daughter of George and Anna Trenholm who died in childhood. Steam powered, sail rigged, and boasting fourteen guns, the *Georgiana* was constructed of heavy iron. Reported to hold over four hundred tons of cargo, she had a clipper bow adorned with the figurehead of a woman. She was described as "the most powerful Confederate cruiser" by Confederate naval officer and historian Thomas Scharf.

On the night of March 19, 1863, the *Georgiana* sailed toward Charleston Harbor. She was laden with ammunition, medicine, sundries, and 350 pounds of gold. While running so close to Federal gunboats that her crew heard orders being called on the Northern vessels, the *Georgiana* was shot through the hull and rudder. Her propeller was so damaged that her captain ran her aground. He and the crew then scuttled her and escaped to shore. When the Federals set her on fire, the explosions and fires lasted for three days, a testament to the tremendous amount of ammunition she carried.

As his fortune increased due to blockade running, Trenholm bought at least $20,000 worth of Confederate bonds—$4 million in today's economy—to help finance the war. But he also helped many whose lives the war had devastated. He donated funds to aid disabled soldiers, both Northern and Southern, and others in need, both black and white. One of his vessels carried to Britain just over $7,000 worth of cotton belonging to the Orphan House Board and returned with $100,000 worth of shoes and clothing for the Charleston Orphan House. He also bought a building in upstate South Carolina for the orphans to stay in when General Beauregard evacuated civilians from Charleston; the children remained there for over two years. Trenholm is believed to have begun the Wayside House and Hospital for soldiers in Charleston. He supplied thousands of Bibles for the Confederates, since few were available in the South.

While Trenholm was generous and helped those in need during the war, he also enjoyed his wealth. Ashley Hall, one of his numerous abodes, was a palatial Charleston residence said to be larger than the governor's mansion. He entertained lavishly there. Even his servants were clothed richly. Trenholm often gave friends rare luxury items nearly impossible to obtain except through blockade running. While military and medical supplies occupied the greatest space on his vessels, there always seemed to be nooks and crannies where European perfume, ladies' kid gloves, silk parasols, sewing silk, children's books, and other smuggled luxuries could be stowed. Trenholm's generosity and lavish lifestyle were made possible not just by the war supplies his blockade runners smuggled, but also by the sale of luxury cargo and nonmilitary items tucked in nearly every shipment. Still, of all the blockade-running companies, Trenholm's dedicated more space to war supplies than any other. Though smuggling civilian luxury items was more lucrative, Fraser, Trenholm & Company remained devoted to its mission to supply the Confederate military. By the end of the war, the company had increased its shipping line from five cargo ships to over sixty steamers and numerous sailing ships.

In August 1863, Trenholm bought five Georgetown rice plantations—Annandale, Beneventum, Tidyman's Marsh, Pine Grove, and Ravenel. In 1864, he obtained Hopeland Plantation.

During the last year of the war, President Jefferson Davis appointed Trenholm as secretary of the treasury. The first treasurer was Christopher Gustavus Memminger. Memminger had embarked upon that difficult task in February 1861, doing his best to guide the finances of the Confederacy, a new nation with no government treasury and a populace that had favored secession mainly to avoid taxation. Due to criticism he received for the failing Confederate economy, Memminger resigned on July 18, 1863.

Trenholm was appointed the same day Memminger withdrew. A better secretary of the treasury could not have been found. Trenholm, after all, was the South's banking liaison with its financial allies in Britain. And Fraser, Trenholm & Company was the Confederacy's financial agent in Europe.

If anyone could have turned the South's finances around, Trenholm was the man. But it was too late. His personal purchase of Confederate war bonds is believed to have kept the war going. Despite his efforts to increase government revenue by levying taxes, soliciting donations, and urging that stored cotton be shipped to Britain for military credit, rescuing the South's failing economy was an impossible task.

Unable to reverse the failing economy, Trenholm had in effect joined President Davis's Cabinet just in time to be punished by Federal officials. He held his post in Richmond, Virginia, from the time of his appointment until April 1865, when the government fell.

On April 2, when Richmond was captured by Federal troops, President Davis and his Cabinet—with the exception of Secretary of War John Breckenridge—evacuated on a train bound for Danville, Virginia. The capital was in effect moved farther south to a city that had not fallen. The train also carried everything moveable that comprised the capital, including the treasury. According to some estimates, it transported the equivalent of, in today's terms, $1 billion in donated jewelry and government gold and silver. Trenholm was on the train. Accompanying him was his wife, Anna, the only lady among the approximately thirty men.

Trenholm's role in the last days of the treasury's known whereabouts and in its disappearance is not clear. What exactly happened to all that gold, silver, and jewelry? The accounts are many and varied.

It is known that Trenholm demanded the treasury be shipped out of Richmond on the train to Danville. As head of the war's most successful blockade-running business, he was the best choice to spirit it to safety.

The train crossed numerous trestles—including the one spanning the Dan River—and made a number of stops, each of which has been proposed as a drop-off or hiding place for the entirety or portions of the treasury.

After General Robert E. Lee surrendered his army on April 9 at Appomattox, Davis and his Cabinet moved to Greensboro, North Carolina. On a hectic night less than a week later, they headed to Charlotte. The tracks south of Greensboro had been destroyed by Stoneman's Raiders, rendering the train useless. Everything from the cars—official papers, government archives, personal baggage, and supposedly the treasury—had to be loaded onto a cavalcade of horse-drawn conveyances. Meanwhile, President Davis worked on plans for reestablishing the capital farther south.

On the way to Charlotte, Trenholm and his wife walked in mud that was nearly ankle deep. Next, they rode in an open horse-drawn ambulance, where Trenholm became violently ill.

Records indicate it was in Charlotte that the actual breakup of the Confederate government occurred, in the home of William Phifer on North Tryon Street. According to Phifer family records, Trenholm, under a doctor's care, was unable to leave his sickbed in the Phifer home, and the last meeting was held by his bedside.

Charlotte remained the Confederate capital until near the end of April, when the remaining Confederate forces in the East surrendered. The cavalcade then traveled into South Carolina, where Trenholm, still ill, resigned as treasurer. He and his wife then headed for Abbeville, where they reunited with their daughters.

Other historians say the last Cabinet meeting was May 5. According to this version, while fleeing Federal troops, Major Raphael J. Moses, General James Longstreet's commissary officer, was given possession of the last of the silver and gold bullion—forty thousand dollars' worth. Moses was told by President Davis to give the bullion to the Southern troops struggling home defeated, exhausted, ill, and hungry. Major Moses fulfilled that duty and even obtained receipts. He was aided by several armed guards, as mobs attempted to take the bullion before it could be given to the weary soldiers.

Still others say the final Cabinet meeting was near Washington, Georgia, where Secretary of War John C. Breckenridge of Kentucky and Secretary of State Judah P. Benjamin of Louisiana separated from Davis to head for Florida by different routes, after which they intended to flee the country. Residents of Washington, Georgia, and surrounding Wilkes County have claimed in years hence that heavy rains wash up gold coins on dirt roads near Chenault Plantation.

Other say the treasury became the Mumford Endowment, used for scholarship legacies for orphans in the town of Waynesville, Georgia, in Brantley County. According to this account, the treasury was smuggled to England by Sylvester Mumford, who deposited it in a bank and then brought it back to Waynesville.

Still others say the treasury was taken to Canada to be hidden by Confederate operatives there.

Most historians agree that when Davis, the remaining Cabinet members, and the rest of the entourage were captured in Irwinville, Georgia, after crossing the Savannah River, the treasury was gone. Others say a small portion was captured with Davis.

But could the treasury have been spirited away to safety by possibly the greatest smuggler of all time, George Alfred Trenholm, the mastermind behind his company's successful blockade running throughout the war?

After leaving Richmond, the train bearing the Confederate government and the treasury rolled over trestles spanning deep rivers. Many believe Trenholm dropped the treasury into the rivers. After all, his son William Lee Trenholm patented an underwater metal detector, the Hypohydroscope—United States patent number 269139—after the war.

In the meantime, Trenholm and his family found a Columbia, South Carolina, house to live in. Their own Columbia home, a beautiful villa named De Greffin after a Trenholm ancestor, had been searched out and burned by seven Federal soldiers, five of whom left their names behind the door of the only part of the property not in ruins.

Despite his dire circumstances, Trenholm never considered fleeing the country.

"One handful of the ashes of our ruined city," he wrote of Charleston, "is more dear to me than all the broad acres of foreign lands."

He had committed no crime and had tremendous responsibilities at home in South Carolina. He had his large family of wife, children, sons- and daughters-in-law, and grandchildren. He had the responsibility of the newly freed slaves on his six Georgetown County rice plantations. He had his business to rebuild. Besides, he could not abandon the vulnerable, newly fallen South.

"And my country, come what will," he wrote, "remains dearer to me than all the world besides."

Trenholm knew he was sought by United States officials on charges related to his blockade running. Hoping to resolve the matter, he headed for Charleston to turn himself over to Federal authorities, who insinuated he would receive clemency for cooperating. Instead, Trenholm was met at the Charleston train depot by officials who roughly seized him and threw him in jail.

Trenholm's arrest was on June 13, 1865, two months after Richmond fell. Five days later, he was moved to Fort Pulaski in Georgia. On June 25, he was paroled. He returned to Charleston, where on July 12 he was once again arrested. He was held in prison until October 14.

In the weeks and months following the war's end, Trenholm was accused of setting up his branch office in Britain to aid the Confederacy. His accusers disregarded the fact that Trenholm had been in the import-export business with Britain and other countries for decades and that Britain was the home of his largest customers.

Trenholm, the United States government claimed, owed tariffs on all the goods brought into Southern ports by his ships from the time the Confederacy seceded until his last ship ran the blockade. In reparation, officials seized over a hundred of his properties, including a tremendous amount of real estate.

Accused, arrested, incarcerated, then freed—though this series of events befell him twice in 1865, Trenholm never confessed. Having operated within the laws of the legally seceded Confederate States of America, he felt he had no crimes to admit to. He requested, via letter, a pardon from President Andrew Johnson so that he might legally hire the freedmen who were looking to him as a source of employment for their families' livelihoods. A letter requesting a pardon for Trenholm was also written by his minister. Petitions in his behalf were signed by a number of Federal generals. President Johnson officially pardoned Trenholm soon afterward.

Though seriously ill while in prison, Trenholm was mainly concerned for his family. Early in their marriage, he and his wife had suffered the deaths of their first four children in infancy. After that, the Trenholms had eight children who lived to adulthood. Trenholm was determined that those sons and daughters and their families should have homes. He wrote to his children from prison, encouraging them in the direction of agriculture on the properties he had managed to save. Agricultural endeavors, he knew, would not only provide them with livelihoods but also make available the same for the freed slaves who were looking to him for help.

In December 1865, Trenholm deeded Annandale Plantation to his son-in-law William Miles Hazzard, a Confederate scout whom Trenholm's daughter Emily St. Pierre had married in January 1864. In 1866, he also deeded Beneventum Plantation to Hazzard. Tidyman's Marsh Plantation remained in the family and was later combined with Annandale, where Hazzard planted rice until the late 1890s. In 1868, Trenholm set up a trust including Hopeland Plantation for his daughter-in-law Kate and her children. Since Kate's husband, Trenholm's son William Lee, was so deeply in debt, the trust was reserved for taking care of the family and educating the children, rather than paying William's debts. Kate and the children would be the beneficiaries of the trust, with William as a trustee. Before his 1876 death, Trenholm deeded Ravenel and Pine Grove plantations to his son Alfred Glover Trenholm.

Most of Trenholm's other properties were confiscated. To justify the confiscations, prosecutors charged that Trenholm had failed to pay United States customs duty on everything he had brought into the South while running the Federal blockade.

Through its Liverpool office, Fraser, Trenholm & Company had aided the Confederacy more than any other blockade-running business. For Britain's role in the endeavor, the American government insisted it pay for damages done to the United States by shipments from England to the Confederacy, for damages caused by allowing Confederate ships to use British ports, and for damages done by Confederate ships built in British shipyards.

The government insisted Britain make reparation by giving Canada to the United States. Although that did not come about, the United States did receive £3 million in the Alabama Claim, a lawsuit concerning damage done to United States Navy ships by the British-built CSS *Alabama*. The *Alabama*, of course, would never have been built without Fraser, Trenholm & Company's aid in smoothing the way for her construction, launching, and outfitting.

Trenholm cared deeply about his South Carolina Low Country homeland and those who lived there. He donated generously to both black and white families and to orphans and soldiers whose lives had been altered by the war. His wife became chairperson of a group devoted to providing postwar help for thousands of destitute people, particularly women, not reached by public charities.

In a letter to one of his business partners in Britain, Trenholm wrote that even before war's end, he had been convinced that the emancipation of the slaves was necessary no matter who won. In October 1865, while still in prison at Fort Pulaski, Georgia, he wrote that "every effort should be made to uplift the blacks."

Ever the innovative and shrewd shipping magnate, Trenholm renewed his ties with the railroad. In 1842, he was elected to a lifetime post as director of the South Carolina Railroad. He also became director of the Blue Ridge Railroad when it reorganized in 1868. Hoping to connect Charleston with the Midwest, he worked diligently to have that railroad built. But after major construction, including tunnel excavation, had been partially completed in four states, a corrupt official embezzled the Blue Ridge Railroad's assets and headed north.

To this day, many believe that Trenholm kept the Confederate treasury safely hidden, biding his time until Reconstruction ended.

During Reconstruction, he saw South Carolina's state debt triple under Robert Kingston Scott, governor from 1868 to 1872, despite the general assembly's unsuccessful effort to impeach the Northern native. In 1868, the term for South Carolina governors was extended, allowing Scott four years to misuse the state's funds, instead of only two. In fact, Scott later moved to Ohio when Democratic power was restored in the South Carolina government, probably fearing prosecution for misuse of funds.

No wonder Trenholm, if he had the treasury, did not restore it during Scott's administration!

Trenholm passed away in Charleston in his seventieth year on December 9, 1876, eleven and a half years after the war's end.

In October 1876, a South Carolina Democrat was at last elected governor. Former Confederate general Wade Hampton, despite sore opposition from the Reconstruction Republicans, won the election. Hampton gave a speech on December 7, just two days before Trenholm's death, in which he vowed to uphold his rightfully elected seat.

The following year, Reconstruction ended with the withdrawal of United States troops. Democrats returned to power that same year. It was too late for Trenholm to reveal the hidden treasury—if he had it. We may never know.

Jefferson Davis once stated, referring to Trenholm, "No consideration of personal danger ever caused him to swerve from the path of duty."

Had Trenholm lived just a short time longer, would he have retrieved the missing treasury—provided he ever had it—and sought to finance a true reconstruction using the financial genius that was forced into dormancy after the war?

Waiting for Reconstruction to end, did Trenholm take the treasury's hidden location to his grave?

With so many of his properties seized after the war, what would he have considered a safe hiding place?

Many of his Charleston properties were confiscated, but he made a point of keeping his six Georgetown rice plantations in the family. Was—is—the balance of the treasury hidden on one of them?

Is it buried within sight of the huge white columns of Annandale's palatial mansion, later renamed Millbrook, where daughter Emily St. Pierre and her husband, Captain Hazzard, lived? Or near the rice fields of Beneventum or Tidyman's Marsh, where they continued to grow rice after the war?

Is it secreted deep beneath the evergreens on Ravenel—later renamed Rochelle—or Pine Grove, the plantations deeded to son Alfred Glover?

Did son William Lee invent the Hypohydroscope for retrieving the treasury from the bottom of one of the rivers the treasure-bearing train and then the wagon cavalcade crossed in 1865? If so, the missing fortune may lie buried on Hopeland Plantation, where William Lee and his family lived.

Even now, the treasury may still be out there waiting—right where George Alfred Trenholm left it.

Victorian Coffin Bells

Saved by the bell.
That rings a bell.
Graveyard shift.

These three phrases have the same origin—Victorian coffin bells.

The quaint custom of the coffin bell became obsolete well over a century ago. During the nineteenth century, however, the bells offered blessed peace of mind to the bereaved of Victorian-era Georgetown.

During the Victorian years, a grave concern was the fear of being buried while still living. That concern was spurred by rare occurrences of seemingly dead individuals reviving prior to burial. Those incidents, though uncommon, led to an awful question—what if the supposedly deceased revived *after* burial?

Modern medical practices assure that could *never* happen nowadays. Modern burial practices doubly assure it. But burial alive was a possibility in the 1800s. Nineteenth-century medical care left a greater margin for error. Comas were sometimes mistaken for death. Catalepsy, a frequent side effect of schizophrenia prior to the advent of modern drug treatments, produced a trancelike catatonic state during which its sufferers appeared dead. Victims of highly contagious diseases such as diphtheria, smallpox, cholera, measles, scarlet fever, and typhoid fever were hastily buried to prevent the spread of the disease. Most of the victims passed away at home and were pronounced dead by family members, rather than by an attending physician. By law, the physician who signed the death certificate did not have to personally examine the alleged deceased. The doctor could sign after being *told* the victim was dead.

The possibility of live burial worried some people to no end. To assure their peace of mind, numerous coffin alarm devices, most featuring a bell, were patented from the mid-1800s through the early 1900s. By far the most widely used coffin bell alarm was Bateson's Life Revival Device, also known simply as Bateson's Belfry. Invented by George Bateson, it assured that should the deceased awaken after burial, he would have the means to ring for help.

"A most economical, ingenious, and trustworthy mechanism, superior to any other method, and promoting peace of mind amongst the bereaved in all stations of life. A device of proven efficacy, in countless instances in this country and abroad," read Bateson's advertisement.

During the Victorian age, Bateson's Belfries and other coffin bell alarms adorned many of the new graves in cemeteries far and wide. Georgetown County was no exception. In at least two instances in South Carolina—one in Beaufort and one in Newberry—a supposedly dead fever victim revived *after* being interred above ground in the family crypt.

Since fever deaths occurred in Georgetown County, it was natural that some new graves here were graced with Victorian coffin bells.

The coffin bell device was easily recognizable. Visible at the head of the grave was a curious-looking pipe with a sheltered cover at the top containing a small bell. *Not* visible was the rest of the device. A string was attached to the bell. The string ran down the pipe—sometimes referred to as a "breathing tube"—and into the coffin, where it was attached to the ring finger of the deceased.

Theoretically, should the deceased turn out not to be dead after all but in a coma or catatonic state, he would be *saved by the bell*. Any movement of his hand would ring the bell above—*That rings a bell*—alerting the listener posted in the cemetery. Listeners worked shifts—*graveyard shifts*—for the first few weeks following burial.

After several weeks had passed, the bell and pipe were more often than not removed by the undertaker and saved until requested for another new grave. Very few bells remained indefinitely on graves.

The cemeteries of Georgetown County, many containing graves dating back to the eighteenth century, are for the most part carefully groomed. Nowadays, no trace of a coffin bell is known to remain on any Georgetown grave. The transitory pipes, strings, and bells of nineteenth-century coffin alarm devices were long ago removed from grave sites. Any pipe not removed would have rusted away long ago, allowing the bell to drop to the ground.

Some old cemeteries in remote areas, however, have fallen into disrepair, especially when the accompanying churches no longer exist. Such is the circumstance of the cemetery of Old Pee Dee Methodist Church in western Georgetown County. Most of the people buried there were interred during the nineteenth century.

With the Old Pee Dee Methodist Church long gone, the burial ground has been growing wild for many years. The low wrought-iron fence surrounding it is barely visible because of overgrown shrubs and hedges. A deep blanket of pine and cedar needles assures that no grass ever needs to be cut. Towering evergreen trees have grown up through many of the graves. Large poisonous snakes are quite at home here, should anyone chance to wander through.

Such is an environment in which a coffin bell might remain for many years. The death dates of family members noted on headstones in the cemetery indicate that many perished close together, which suggests that a number of those buried here were victims of contagious fevers. Death from such illnesses prompted hasty burial—and sometimes a coffin bell. It was rumored in the late 1990s that coffin alarm bells had survived intact in the ancient churchyard. However, any remaining bells were long gone when this author thoroughly explored the churchyard while researching this book.

The Bateson's Life Revival Device was so popular that George Bateson became wealthy from its sales. However, no record of burial alive has ever been recorded in Georgetown. It is safe to assume that no coffin bell was ever rung here by a buried person. The only time the coffin bells rang was when being installed on new graves and then again when being removed weeks or years later.

Ghostly ringing, however, is a different story. Though the coffin bells are long gone, the eerie tinkle of their placement and removal remains.

The reverent silence pervading Georgetown County's ancient live-oak-shaded country cemeteries is usually broken only by birdsong from the treetops. In the churchyard cemeteries in town, the birds are hourly eclipsed by the tolling from the bell towers.

Sometimes, though, the tiny, distinct tinkle of a bell from long ago chimes among Georgetown's ancient gravestones. This pure, clear ring, sometimes only a sharp tinkle or two, is the ghostly sound of the placing or removal of quaint old precautionary Victorian coffin bells.

Serpents

Many and legendary are the superstitions in Georgetown County concerning the long, mysterious reptiles that slither silently through the summer months.

Occasionally glimpsed in town, these furtive creatures are more at home roaming remote areas of the county. Serpents are sometimes found lying languidly upon the moss-draped, low-hanging limbs of the black cypress and live oak trees lining Georgetown's dark, winding rivers. Oftentimes, a wide, straight stretch of river will be broken only by the narrow wake of a snake swimming surreptitiously from one bank to the other.

Whether quietly harmless or deadly venomous, snakes have been the subjects of superstitious beliefs in Georgetown County since the early nineteenth century.

During the 1920s, sociologist and folklorist Dr. Newbell Niles Puckett spent time in Georgetown County research-ing beliefs and superstitions. A professor at Western Reserve

University in Cleveland, Ohio, Dr. Puckett researched and recorded over a hundred eighteenth- and nineteenth-century folk ballads and lumber-camp songs in Ontario and was working on a collection of Ohio folklore when he died. He is best known, however, for his work in Southern black folklore. While researching *Folk Beliefs of the Southern Negro*, published in 1926 by the University of North Carolina Press, he collected from Georgetown County, other parts of South Carolina, and other Southern states at least ten thousand beliefs and superstitions, many of which had never been recorded. Many of them were about snakes.

Long ago in Georgetown County, it was believed that a snake could grasp the end of its tail with its mouth to form a wheel or hoop. In that form, it was believed, the snake could roll faster than it could slither—and faster than a person could run.

Anyone running from a snake was advised to keep a straight path, for it was said a snake could not follow a direct track without coiling. Running straight could buy precious time to escape.

Catching a rattlesnake and rubbing the rattles on your eyes, it was believed, gave you the ability to always catch sight of a rattlesnake before it caught sight of you.

A wavy snake trail in the dust of a dirt road, it was believed, indicated a poisonous snake had traveled there, while a straight track was the sign of a harmless one.

If a snake had crossed at the place where *you* were crossing, you would get a backache—unless you walked backwards over the same place.

It was believed that coachwhip snakes could stand straight up and whistle. In fact, it was thought that all snakes communicated with one another by whistling. For that reason, a person walking through the woods should not whistle or else they might be answered by a snake. Also, a person hearing a whistle of unknown origin should never whistle back, as he might unknowingly whistle up a snake!

It was believed that blacksnakes, also known as milk snakes, would milk cows out in the field, sometimes milking them dry. Cows lowing in the field were said to be calling for their milk snakes. The snakes would then wait for the cows in one area of the field. One cow was said to have pined away from grief after her milk snake was killed. On rare occasions, milk snakes were said to have crept into homes to nurse sleeping women. It was also believed that milk snakes could charm children.

Snakes shed their skins annually as they grow longer. The shed skin of a snake was believed to have a special magic and was used for all sorts of reasons.

A snakeskin was usually part of a good-luck mojo consisting of protective ingredients tied up in red flannel.

Rubbing a snakeskin on your hands would keep you from dropping or breaking dishes.

A snakeskin worn around the leg or waist would keep you strong and flexible.

The skin shed by a graveyard snake was believed to be especially potent. Black with yellow patches, graveyard snakes lived in the graveyard, where they could mourn and grieve. When they shed their skins in the graveyard, the discarded skins could be worn around the waist by people wishing to defeat enemies.

Conjure doctors often used snakes in their enchantments. One conjure doctor always had with him a crooked walking stick. When he tossed it on the ground, it would writhe like a snake. Once he picked it up, it was a rigid walking stick once more.

A person who had been conjured or had accidentally ingested a small snake while drinking out of a stream could, it was believed, have terrible troubles with snakes inside the body.

One man never seemed to receive nourishment no matter how much he ate. Hoping for relief, he went to a conjure doctor. The doctor told him he had several small snakes in his body that immediately consumed any food he ate.

Conjure doctors could rid people of snakes inside them. They were able to charm snakes, too.

A snake found in a person's bed was a sign that person had been conjured.

People often wondered if they had been conjured and were sometimes warned of a conjuration attempt by dreams— snake dreams. What did snake dreams indicate?

Dreaming of a snake was an indication of having enemies.

Dreaming of a rattlesnake meant the conjure doctor had a conjure that would work on you. If the snake in the dream attempted to bite you but missed, then the conjure had missed you, too.

Dreaming of a rattlesnake indicated a dangerous conjure, while dreaming of a chicken snake meant only a small sickness.

Dreaming of a snake coiled and ready to strike indicated the conjure doctor was furious with you. But if the snake in your dream was resting quietly, then the conjure doctor was merely thinking about you.

Not documented by Dr. Puckett was the Georgetown County belief that snakes were attracted to expectant mothers. Snakes, it was said, did not seek out pregnant women to do them harm but rather just to be near them. One lady related that during her pregnancy, a snake would slither up onto her porch and remain there until removed.

A tale is told of one expectant mother in Georgetown who was charmed by a blacksnake in her yard. She could not stop staring at the snake and was finally taken, trancelike, into the house by her relatives. Only then did she cease to stare. When her baby was born, the child had rattles beginning to grow on it in the area around its stomach. The rattles were removed by the baby's doctor.

Serpents still roam Georgetown County, so beware of stepping on one! Though the harmless snakes are worth their weight in gold for the many thousands of mosquitoes they eat, the venomous ones are no less worthy of fear and respect than when Dr. Newbell Niles Puckett came to learn the age-old local beliefs.

Sea View Inn

For the better part of a century, folks have been returning every year to Pawleys Island's lofty, rambling Sea View Inn for a delightful sojourn by the Atlantic and three delicious home-cooked meals a day. Some folks are so happy during their stay here that they continue to visit even though their time on earth has passed.

A sprawling two-story wooden lodge built atop high, grass-covered dunes, Sea View Inn rises out of the trees amid tiered wooden walkways and breezy, wood-framed screen porches. A long, old-fashioned back porch opens onto the dining room, where culinary delights are served from the big adjoining kitchen. Boasting twenty ocean-air-cooled guest rooms plus a cottage, the inn has a long, deep, wide, shady plantation veranda on the ocean side, lined with wooden rocking chairs and a quintessential Pawleys Island rope hammock.

Brian Henry of Sea View Inn has compiled a history of the inn and its former owners.

By the 1930s, Pawleys Island was already a place where families returned year after year. It was said that everyone knew everyone else, as well as what house they were staying in. Celeste and Will Clinkscales from Spartanburg were no exception. Celeste was a schoolteacher, and Will, her husband, was a math professor at Duke University. They visited Pawleys Island regularly and considered their family and friends to be "Pawleys people" also.

During the 1930s, Celeste helped run a bed-and-breakfast on Pawleys. So pleased was she with the venture that in 1937, she and Will financed and built Sea View Inn. Celeste, the driving force, ultimately became the hostess of Sea View.

The inn almost immediately established itself as a place where guests returned for the same week in the same room each year—just as is done today. The clientele was intended to be the Clinkscales' friends and family but soon included many regulars who wanted to try the new inn "in the middle of Pawleys Island."

Celeste and Will always sat at a table in a small alcove on the northern side of Sea View's dining room. From there, Celeste, the consummate hostess, frequently rose to converse with guests. Gracious, quiet, and interesting, she could engage people easily. Her genteel and friendly demeanor set the tone for the inn.

Celeste and Will Clinkscales kept Sea View for fifteen years.

In April 1952, the inn was sold to three ladies from Queens College in Charlotte, North Carolina. Miss Thelma Albright was the college's dean of students, Miss Alma Hull was director of guidance, and Miss Loma Squires was the dietician. Miss Thelma and Miss Alma had been going to the inn for the past thirteen years.

In a letter to regular guests dated April 24, 1952,

Thelma, Alma, and Loma announced that they had bought their "favorite vacation spot lock, stock, and both barrels!" They promised that "Miss Loma Squires would attend to your inner satisfaction, while Miss Alma and Miss Thelma would see that your other creature comforts are assured."

Hurricane Hazel struck Pawleys Island in October 1954. The island suffered major damage. Sea View Inn was toppled and destroyed by the storm tide and wind. Its future was in jeopardy.

In a letter dated March 16, 1955, Thelma Albright informed Sea View patrons that the owners were "still smarting a bit from Hazel, and we have not recovered entirely from the shock of seeing the wreckage of Sea View after the hurricane. . . . We are going to be back in business. . . . Our loan has been approved. . . . The plan is essentially the same as the old Sea View. . . . The house is going to be set back a bit farther from the beach."

The main building of Sea View—the same structure that exists today—was completed by 1956. The accompanying cottage remains as well.

Over the years, Loma and Thelma went their separate ways, leaving Alma as sole proprietor of Sea View Inn until 1978.

According to the August-September 1980 issue of the *Pawleys Island Perspective*, "Alma developed some interesting policies during her term. She locked the doors of Sea View promptly at 10 P.M. each evening, and if you were late, that was just too bad. No liquor was served, but some guests brought their own refreshments, which they enjoyed in their own rooms. One gentleman asked Alma if he could get some ice for a drink at 9:30 one evening. Alma replied by calling the man a degenerate!

"On rainy days she pre-addressed post cards to her Congressman and passed them around to guests so that they could write messages.

"There is no doubt that Alma Hull was a character, but she certainly made Sea View become one of the respected inns on the island. Of course, the food helped make that reputation, and if Alma ran the Inn, it was Geneva Polite who was queen of the kitchen, cooking up a storm three times a day."

The next "protector" of Sea View Inn was Page Oberlin, who had come to Pawleys as both a child and an adult. In 1978, she brought her children from Ohio, where she had been running a restaurant. She contacted Alma, who was ill and eager to sell. Page ran Sea View for twenty-four years.

In the spring of 2002, Sassy and Brian Henry took on the role of the new "protectors" of Sea View. Sassy was born and raised in Atlanta and attended Mary Baldwin College in Virginia. She owned and operated a business called the Sassy Tree in the 1990s and had a particular interest and talent in landscape design, holiday home decorating, antiques, and preparing cut-flower and potted-plant arrangements. Already a proficient cook, Sassy worked as a chef's apprentice at an executive dining room for three years, honing her expertise in food preparation and planning. Brian was born and raised in Lafayette, Louisiana, and attended Louisiana State University in Baton Rouge. After moving to Atlanta in 1990, he acquired professional experience with a consulting firm and with Coca-Cola. He and Sassy married in 1997.

Some of Sassy's fondest memories were of walking through Pawleys Creek catching crabs with her dad. Her family had visited Pawleys Island since she was a baby. After vacationing on the island with them, Brian also fell in love with the island of rustic old houses, Atlantic sand, uncrowded beaches, and creek mud.

On Brian and Sassy's second trip together to Pawleys, a family friend mentioned that Sea View Inn was "quietly" for sale. At that time, the Henrys were living just north of downtown Atlanta. Escalating growth, intense competition for private schools, the corporate lifestyle, unbearable traffic, and social climbing already had them considering living in a smaller town. They began to focus their desire for a lifestyle change on the prospect of living on Pawleys Island. Brian and Sassy felt like they "would win the lottery" if they could take advantage of the once-in-a-lifetime opportunity to purchase Sea View. They believed that their combined talents would be ideally suited for such an endeavor.

It was time to get a plan, get answers to important questions, and begin a six-month process of prayer, negotiation, and cipherin' (a Southern term for studyin' and plannin'). The decision to "go for it" led to a memorable first meeting with Page over lunch at the inn in August 2001. Then came numerous phone calls and overnighted proposals. On December 7, they met with Page Oberlin and were informed that they were "the ones." They loaded up their belongings and their two young daughters and headed for Pawleys.

Brian and Sassy have maintained the integrity and ambiance of what has become an institution for many people. Their primary focus has been to refine without changing and to subtly improve with an eye toward historical appreciation.

And appreciated Sea View Inn is—so much so that guests have been moved to return after passing away from this earthly life.

Mrs. Frances, who works at Sea View, related the following experience, told to her by a previous owner.

"A band used to come here and stayed in the whole upstairs. After their last visit, they were going on to Charleston or Columbia, one of those two cities. They had an accident. All of them died. After that, the owner's children were in the living room. The children saw all the men coming down the stairs dressed in tuxedos. They asked their mother why she didn't speak to the men."

The children's mother had seen no one.

Brian Henry related a more recent encounter.

"The instructor for Artists' Week at Sea View Inn had never experienced a ghostly encounter. She didn't really believe in ghosts but was skittish enough to not enjoy ghost stories. They reminded her of her younger years when she would not find her mom home after walking home from school. The young girl knew she needed to practice the piano before walking up the street to her piano lesson with Mrs. Earle, but she would hear crackles and squeaks throughout the house that she never noticed when Mom was home. She would gather her lesson books and huddle on the curb out front of the house until time to go to her lesson.

"Now that the art teacher was an adult, she had put away those sorts of fears. It never occurred to her there might be ghosts at Sea View Inn."

For Artists' Week, Brian put the teacher in the cottage, as he usually did. She had stayed in Room C in the cottage several times and was also familiar with the single bed and writing desk in Room D, the tiny room on the other side of a shared bathroom. At night, the teacher would leave the bathroom light burning and latch the hook of the bathroom door that gave access to Room D.

"As was her habit, she woke up in the middle of the night to use the bathroom," Brian related. "Before getting out of the bed, she heard some bumping around that sounded like someone coming up the steps from the outside boardwalk. She heard them opening the screen door and sliding suitcases across the floor.

" 'Ah,' she thought, 'the night manager has someone with a very late arrival, and he is moving someone into the adjoining room. How nice! I think that was the last empty room in the inn. But now I will have to share my bathroom.'

"The teacher lay still for a few minutes, listening to the newcomer getting settled into the little room. Then her bathroom call was such that she needed to heed that call. When she finished, she carefully unlatched the hook so the new person would have access to their shared bathroom. She then closed the bathroom door leading into her bedroom. Upon settling back in the bed, she distinctly heard the new guest open the bathroom door and lift the lid and seat to the commode."

The teacher then heard the unmistakable sound of a man relieving himself.

"At breakfast the next morning, the teacher congratulated the owner of the inn for filling all his rooms during the off-season by moving a gentleman into D of the cottage. The owner returned a puzzled look and explained that no one had moved into D during the night.

" 'But,' the teacher exclaimed, 'I heard them move into the room. I even heard him go into the bathroom and relieve himself!'

"The daughter of the previous owner overheard the conversation and began to laugh. She explained that George was playing one of his cottage tricks. George Frost, she continued, was a manager at Sea View Inn in the 1980s. He managed the inn during the season. During the winter, which was the off-season, he traveled the world. After leaving Sea View, George stayed in touch with an ongoing regular guest by way of online backgammon. They played every Sunday night. In the weeks prior to George's death, he had not been online for a few weeks, and the guest became concerned. George, confined to a bed at that point, had communicated to the guest just prior to his death that all he wanted to do was return to Sea View Inn one more time."

George had died earlier on the very same day the teacher heard the phantom visitor check in. He apparently made it back for one last night. Room D was George's office during the winter!

But who exactly was George Frost?

When on visits to Sea View Inn during George's tenure as seasonal manager, guest Gene Roberson and his wife, Sandy, came to know and love George. Gene enjoyed many games of backgammon at Sea View with George before becoming his Sunday-night Internet backgammon partner.

"I know far more about who he was then than about his life before we met," wrote Gene. "I know that he had a lifetime love of the sea, and that his favorite time was when he was taking transocean cruises. He preferred to hitch rides on freighters. I think he served in a branch of the Navy that kept him at sea a lot. He had fascinating off-seasons from the Sea View, such as volunteering at an orphanage in Guatemala, working on communication research projects in Hawaii, sailing for weeks to Australia, spending a couple of nights ashore and hopping another ship to return, or working at arts festivals in upper New York State, which was his home. Sandy and I visited him there when he was about eighty-four and found that he was just starting to learn to play the clarinet.

"He was working at Sea View as a manager's assistant in the mid-1980s when we first started going. In fact, he was the first person we met there, and for many years, for us and other guests, he was the face of Sea View. He was soft-spoken and always warm and pleasant. He welcomed each guest as if they had come to visit him. When he wasn't working, he spent most of his time socializing with guests.

"We never go to Sea View without remembering, appreciating, and missing George."

Life's happiest days are the ones we would like most to repeat. That is why some of those who are no longer of this earth choose occasionally to revisit the scenes of some of their happiest days—as George did at Sea View Inn.

Pirates Shipwrecked

In 1735, the *South Carolina Gazette* reported an incident of piracy involving both Georgetown Harbor and Charleston Harbor.

While Charleston was at times rampant with pirate activity, Georgetown was a haven for pirates who hoped to keep lower profiles—and enjoy longer lives. After all, many pirates were publicly hanged in Charleston.

Georgetown's inlets, with their isolated, sandy points and irregular islands, were havens from the open seas yet free from prying eyes. Pirates could remain hidden while working on their vessels or temporarily burying stolen treasure until they could unearth it safely at a later date.

Often, a pirate vessel would slip into Murrells Inlet, just north of Georgetown Harbor, or North Inlet, outside the harbor. There, the crew could anchor and slowly heel their ship over with the receding tide in order to expose one side of the hull for scraping or recaulking the seams. Hours later, the rising tide would right the ship once more.

In the 1735 incident, however, a pirate crew came to Georgetown not to heel their vessel temporarily for maintenance or repair but to deliberately, permanently shipwreck her.

Their misadventure, referenced by Geordie Buxton and Ed Macy in *Haunted Harbor: Charleston's Maritime Ghosts and the Unexplained*, began with a chance meeting one chilly, clammy evening off Sullivan's Island near Charleston. The desperately unhappy crew members of a Spanish ship were sailing the Atlantic, carrying a cargo of Central American silver and gold. They were transporting the fortune home to Spain, risking their lives on the open sea for sailors' wages.

The crew members were wondering how on earth they might keep the treasure for themselves without being caught, tried, and hanged as pirates by the Spanish government when, as fate would have it, a storm drove them toward the coast of South Carolina. After the storm, the fog was so dense that they anchored off Breach Inlet in the Sullivan's Island channel near Charleston.

The crew of the Spanish ship had their treasure-keeping hopes abruptly addressed when their ship was approached in the thick-as-pea-soup fog. Looming upon them out of the mist was a huge, dark, menacing sight. It was no apparition. Bearing down upon them was a pirate corsair, manned by none other than a crew of fearsome Brethren of the Sea! Fearing they were about to be forcibly relieved of their cargo of riches, the Spanish crew rushed to their defensive posts to guard their vessel as the pirate ship came alongside.

They need not have panicked. The pirate crew, from St. Augustine, wanted the treasure, but not by force. They desired to divide the Central American gold and silver with the crew of the Spanish ship while giving the Spanish crew the perfect alibi—they were attacked by pirates!

It did not take the crew of the Spanish ship long to unanimously accept the proposal from their new acquaintances. Anchored alongside one another and rafted together, the Spanish ship and the pirate corsair rocked gently in the fog as the crews laid their plans. There in the deep mist, in what appeared to be secrecy, the two crews plotted a strategy to steal the entire cargo of treasure from the Spanish government.

Little did they know that a Charleston Harbor pilot boat, passing in silence nearby, had spotted the two vessels. The captain of the pilot boat knew that a disabled ship sometimes was rafted to an able vessel until she made port or until help arrived. Checking to see if one of the two vessels was in distress, he approached them unseen in the fog and, along with a merchant vessel passing nearby, overheard their plans. The pilot boat and the merchant ship then sailed into Charleston Harbor and notified authorities as soon as they reached port.

In the meantime, the Spanish ship was to sail north to Georgetown when the fog lifted. In accordance with their plan, the crew would deliberately wreck their vessel off Georgetown Harbor. The pirate crew was then to sail their corsair to Georgetown two days later, pick up the crew from the Spanish ship, and sail them south to Long Island—now the Isle of Palms—off Charleston, where the two crews would divide the stolen gold and silver.

As the fog burned away the next morning, the Spanish ship sailed north toward Georgetown Harbor, clearing the Charleston area just before a sudden, fierce thunderstorm ravaged the ocean for miles around. The pirate crew was not so fortunate. Holding back to give the Spanish ship lead time, they were caught in the thunderstorm. It was over in a few hours, but not before it spawned waterspouts that drove the pirates' corsair and slammed her onto Morris Island, destroying the ship and killing all aboard.

Three days later, the crew of the deliberately wrecked Spanish vessel waited in vain under a brilliant blue sky off Georgetown Harbor. For hours on end, they scanned the southern horizon for the pirate corsair that would never sail again.

Several days after that, authorities in Georgetown, alerted by Charleston authorities, caught the stranded Spanish crew when they attempted to find water to drink on a Georgetown rice plantation.

But what of the cargo of gold and silver? Where off Georgetown Harbor did the Spanish crew choose to wreck their vessel? Could the gold and silver lie buried there? Or was it already buried farther south on Long Island, where the division of the treasure was to take place?

The ill-fated pirates whose corsair shipwrecked on Morris Island never had a chance to retrieve the hidden Spanish treasure. But what became of the Spanish crew?

History has not revealed the fate of the Spanish crew after they were caught in Georgetown. Were they sent to Charleston and hanged as pirates at White Point, as so many Brethren of the Sea were? Or did they live to retrieve their stolen treasure?

Does their fortune in Central American gold and silver lie waiting beneath the sand of an island outside Georgetown Harbor?

Asylum

It is quite natural for a haunting to last many years, then abruptly stop. When this happens, the reason for the haunting has passed. In the case of Asylum Plantation, located in the Plantersville community of Georgetown County, the ghost finished making her point and ceased to haunt. She has not been seen for over half a century—as far as we know.

Plantersville was named for the numerous rice planters who owned and operated plantations there. In the early to mid-nineteenth century, Plantersville was a remote Pee Dee River community consisting of wealthy rice planters, their families, and hundreds of slaves. Its isolation gave rise to numerous hauntings. Asylum Plantation was the site of one of these.

The originator of Asylum Plantation was Davison McDowell of Ireland. His father, James, had emigrated here and settled near the Pee Dee River in Georgetown in 1786 but died in 1787. His mother, Agnes, had emigrated shortly after her husband passed away and stayed on, later marrying Robert Kirkpatrick.

Young Davison McDowell, born in 1783, had remained in Ireland with relatives to complete his education. He arrived in Georgetown from Newry, Ireland, in 1811 at age twenty-eight and immediately set about becoming a rice planter. Within a year of his arrival, he was well into the business, planting with and renting from fellow planters. He continued in that manner until 1819, when he bought the land that was to become Asylum Plantation, a place of retreat and security.

McDowell kept a journal until 1833, documenting a great deal of life at Asylum. According to his January 1, 1819, entry, he paid $1904.75 for the Pee Dee River property. He bought it from Moses Myers, the first Jewish attorney to be admitted to the bar in South Carolina.

McDowell's rice plantation included 220 acres of highlands and 200 acres of swamp. For part of Asylum's work force, he hired slaves from the plantation of his mother, Agnes Kirkpatrick. Of those slaves, at least four were natives of Africa, including Manza, who was born in 1770. Manza became McDowell's main driver in charge of Asylum's rice-field work force. He and another driver, Sam, were recorded yearly on McDowell's slave lists. Slave drivers, usually slaves themselves such as Manza and Sam, were often hard and unyielding.

McDowell married Mary Moore in 1822 but became a widower in 1823. After Mary's death, he hired an overseer, Samuel Smith, for $150 per year. He instructed Smith "to obey me in all things, to treat my people with humanity during my absence; & to do the best you can for my Interest according to the best of your Judgement & abilities."

According to his journal, McDowell paid taxes on

eighty-four slaves in 1826, one hundred ten slaves in 1829, one hundred seven slaves in 1830, and one hundred thirteen slaves in 1832.

He married again in 1827, this time to a widow, and gained ownership of twenty-one more slaves. That same year, he was bedridden for three weeks with a dreaded fever. He wrote in his journal, "During this month the business of the Plantation went on under the sole direction of Manza. For it pleased the almighty to afflict me with a grievous illness . . . a grievous sickness which the Doctor's called Epidemic."

During McDowell's illness, an event occurred that caused Asylum to be haunted for the next hundred years.

One night, hungry and tired, a slave woman hurried through the gathering darkness on Asylum Plantation. She could hear frogs croaking in the trees, ready to feast on mosquitoes. Her stomach growled ominously, almost drowning out the frogs.

She knew she was late for supper. All the other field hands had already gone back toward the cookhouse. She had been on her way with them until she realized her kerchief was gone. She knew she ought to wait until the next day in the hope of finding it when she went back to the rice field, but she hated to take such a chance. It was her favorite kerchief, blue gingham with a tiny, darker blue flower in each little square, and she wanted to retrieve it that night so she would not have to worry about it. Carefully, she scanned the path, retracing her steps to the field. The kerchief would be hard to see in the dimming twilight.

She was almost back to the field when she slowed dejectedly. She had retraced nearly all her steps, and still no kerchief. She knew the kerchief had been on her head when she left the field, because she had pushed it back just a little when she brushed her hand across her damp brow.

When she reached the earthen trunk surrounding the

field, she climbed up, slowly walked the few feet to the place where she had left the field, and shook her head, sighing. This was where she had last touched her kerchief, and it wasn't lying on the ground. Where could it have fallen?

She heard the unmistakable booming bass grunt of a bull alligator in the river nearby. He must be hungry, too. Her stomach gave a long growl as she turned to leave. Her hand reached up automatically to push back the low-hanging chinaberry branch she had ducked under when she left the field, and there it was! Her kerchief was caught in the low twigs of the branch!

Thankfully, she snatched her kerchief, ran down the earthen trunk, hopped to the ground, and raced for the cookhouse. As soon as she began to run, a pain shot through the front of her thigh. Immediately, she slowed down. It was a long time since she had run flat out, and she was too old for that. She hurried though the dark, limping now. Her stomach growled out loud.

At last, the lights of the cookhouse were in sight. She could see the women outside washing the tin plates in the big, round tin tub.

Her heart sank. The meal had ended. Even if there was any food left, supper was over. The driver never allowed anyone to eat supper late. When suppertime was over, eating was over—no exceptions. Her only supper now might be a pear or two from the big tree near the slave street, but raw pears might not sit well on her empty stomach.

One of the cookhouse workers finished washing plates and picked up a medium-sized cast-iron cauldron. She poured its contents into a larger cauldron that was sitting on the ground. Then she began washing the medium-sized cauldron in the tin washtub.

As the slave woman drew closer, her stomach growled long and low. The smell of crusty cornbread still hung in the humid air. She could smell hominy too, and field peas.

As she neared the tin washtub, she could see the heavy black cast-iron pans in which the cornbread had been cooked. By the light of the hanging kerosene lanterns, she could see a thin layer of crunchy crumbs clinging to the inside of each pan where the batter had risen and baked. Not a crust remained. Her stomach rumbled again.

The smell of hominy and field peas wafted to her. She peered into the big, round cauldron into which she had seen the woman pouring something. The bottom of the cauldron was filled with hominy, with the big dipping spoon still in it! On top of the hominy, the cookhouse woman had poured field peas.

The slave woman's stomach growled again. She was so hungry, and she loved field peas and hominy. She looked around.

The driver would have a fit, she knew, if he saw her eating after mealtime, but he was nowhere to be seen. The overseer would have a fit, too, but he also was out of sight. She knew the master would never want her or any of his people to go hungry. Unfortunately, the master mostly left everything in the hands of the overseer and the driver, or sometimes just the driver.

Quickly, she picked up a newly washed plate and spoon. Out of the corner of her eye, she saw two big, heavy boots appear beside the cauldron. One of the boots reared back and kicked it. Over the cauldron went, spilling the hominy and field peas onto the ground right in front of the hungry woman.

She looked up in surprise.

"Supper is *over*, old woman," the driver scowled. Behind him, the overseer nodded. They turned to walk away.

The woman's eyes flashed angrily. Clenching the plate in one hand, she looked first at the driver, then at the overseer. Where was the master at times like this? He owned several plantations—why couldn't he be here tonight? Asylum Plantation needed a new master, and if that one wasn't any better, then another, or another, or another!

She threw down the plate.

The driver and the overseer turned around. The woman narrowed her eyes. Her nostrils flared. Her voice, full of fury, sounded like icy thunder.

"This plantation will never be held by one owner for very long, I swear it!" she shouted.

The driver and the overseer glanced at one another, then back at the woman.

Eyes blazing, she stared at them a moment, then whirled and stalked away, her malediction still hanging in the air.

The driver and the overseer looked at the overturned cauldron and the food lying ruined on the ground.

"We might ought to have let her eat some supper," said the overseer.

Little did they know the repercussion the night's events would have on the future of Asylum.

Nine years later, the old woman's words began to ring true when Asylum was sold.

Davison McDowell owned additional rice plantations in both Plantersville and other sections of Georgetown County—Rice Hope, Strawberry Hill, Springfield, Pee Dee, Oatlands, Sandy Island, and Woodlands. In 1836, he sold Asylum to Dr. Paul Weston and moved to another of his Pee Dee River plantations, which he named Lucknow.

Following that sale, Asylum went through a succession of more than a dozen owners. When the old slave woman died, her ghost began to appear to slaves at Asylum as the plantation changed hands over and over again.

Dr. Paul Weston willed the plantation to Francis Weston, who sold it to Robert F. W. Allston in 1843. Allston sold it to Cleland C. Huger 1846. Huger conveyed it back to Robert F. W. Allston in 1853. Allston, South Carolina's governor from 1856 to 1858, died and willed it to daughter Elizabeth Waties Allston Pringle in 1864. Her brother, Charles Petigru Allston, bought the plantation in 1869 and operated it with his brother Benjamin until 1878. Benjamin Allston conveyed his portion to Elizabeth C. Ford in 1887, while Charles Petigru Allston conveyed his portion to the Guendalos Rice Company—owned by James Louis LaBruce, Francis Williams Lachicotte, and Louis Claude Lachicotte—in 1899. James Louis LaBruce bought out his partners' interests in 1904. James Louis LaBruce, Jr., and George Albert LaBruce inherited it in 1915. After that, the property was conveyed to Delaware native Thomas G. Samworth, the first editor of *American Rifleman* and the publisher of hunting and small-arms books.

Throughout that time, the ghostly appearances of the slave woman continued. She would, it was said, climb the stairs of the plantation house and tap you on the shoulder while you were sleeping. Without warning, she would materialize in the presence of folks coming back from the rice fields or working in the kitchen building. Workers on Asylum became used to her sudden appearances. They knew she was only checking to make sure they were well fed— and gloating over the frequent exchange of ownership of Asylum.

Over the years, Asylum Plantation changed hands so many times that it began to be called Exchange Plantation. The name stuck.

The chain of ownership ended in 1945, when Exchange Plantation was sold by Thomas G. Samworth to the family that still owns it.

The slave woman's ghost lifted the malediction. Over a century of haunting the plantation was apparently enough. In 1945, she ceased to visit Asylum and has not been seen again—as far as we know.

The Strand Theatre

Theaters hold a special place in the hearts of many. They are unique venues where anything can, and just might, happen.

With its fanciful Art Deco marquee and façade, Georgetown's historic Strand Theatre was designed long ago to transport movie audiences past the realm of the expected. Sometimes, however, the *actors* are the recipients of the unexpected.

Movie theaters have been a tradition in Georgetown's downtown historic district for the past century, beginning in 1909 with the Air Dome Theatre, a platform covered in iron at 718 Front Street. A roof was added to the Air Dome in 1910 to protect audiences from the elements.

The same gentleman who owned the Air Dome opened the Electric Theatre at 810 Front Street. The Electric Theatre is believed to have closed by 1913.

In May 1914, the Princess Theatre opened at 628 Front Street and showed movies until it burned down two and a half years later.

In June 1914, the Peerless Theatre opened on what is now the site of the Strand Theatre at 710 Front Street. The Peerless soon closed but was reopened under the name Princess Theatre after the original Princess burned in October 1916. When the theater was sold around 1929, its name was changed back to the Peerless Theatre.

Around 1920, the Palmetto Theatre opened on nearby King Street for African-American patrons. King Oliver and Band, featuring Louis Armstrong on cornet, played a dance there in May 1936 with the balcony kept open for white spectators. The Palmetto Theatre operated until around 1936.

In 1941, the Strand Theatre opened with _Blossoms in the Dust_, starring Greer Garson and Walter Pidgeon. It closed at the end of October 1963 and reopened in January 1964. During the 1970s, the Strand was closed as a movie theater.

In 1971, the Swamp Fox Players theater group organized. They began holding performances in a variety of venues, beginning with the old Winyah High School auditorium.

"We were a wandering troupe at first—hotels, high schools, then the old armory upstairs until it burned down," said Inge Ebert, who has been a member of the Swamp Fox Players for over thirty years.

For a decade, the Swamp Fox Players held performances in a variety of borrowed venues. In June 1982, they bought the Strand Theatre and began its renovation and restoration.

"It had been closed for quite a while. It was moldy and mildewy," said Ebert.

The presences in the old theater were noticeable early on. Footsteps were sometimes heard, but mostly it was just the unmistakable sound of something _there_. Unexplainable sounds came from the balcony and behind the stage.

"We could hear it backstage," Ebert said, "weird noises that were completely inexplicable. When we were backstage, it was really spooky."

The balcony was closed, and the Swamp Fox Players left it that way in the beginning while they concentrated on the ground-floor main theater. Yet they could hear something in the balcony when they knew no one was up there. Later, when they began to open the balcony, the sound continued.

Swamp Fox Player Jo Camlin described the phenomenon: "If we were backstage, we could hear it in the balcony. If we were in the balcony, we could hear it backstage."

"When you were downstairs, you could hear someone going up there *and* walking up there," said Ebert.

No one knew of any ghost associated with the theater, so the presence was a mystery.

"It was an old movie theater," said Ebert. "I'm sure we disturbed whoever was there."

After the Swamp Fox Players completed the restoration of the theater's original marquee, the Strand looked much as it had on opening night in 1941. This effect was heightened by the 1940s-style box office built into the lobby for the movie *Made in Heaven*. The presences that haunt the Strand, however, are from much farther back in Georgetown's past.

One night in 1989, the presences were more strongly felt than ever and demanded to be noticed.

It was in the evening following a performance of the Swamp Fox Players' highly popular production of *Ghosts of the Coast* that the nature of the presences became vividly apparent. During *Ghosts of the Coast*, the actors portrayed people who lived in the area long ago and died very passionate deaths that resulted in the ghostly history for which Georgetown is famous.

One of the actors—who asked that his name not be

used—related the following experience.

"On a July evening in 1989, we four cast members had another well-attended performance. Our play enacting Georgetown ghost legends was performed twice a week at the Strand and had become a big summertime tourist attraction, pulling standing-room-only crowds from vacationing families from as far away as Myrtle Beach.

"Part of the play's appeal was its authenticity. We opened on a dark stage with the audio of a recent *CBS Evening News* story that identified Georgetown as 'the ghost capital of the South.' In our script, we had used authentic Gullah language for the narration and had held close to the version of each legend that Julian Stevenson Bolick had included in his marvelous little book, *Ghosts from the Coast*. We had grown up with the stories Mr. Bolick collected and considered it good, spooky fun to reenact them on stage for tolerant parents and delightedly frightened youngsters. We had even included a segment on Dr. Buzzard, a real-life practitioner of root magic who had lived in the Beaufort, South Carolina, area in the early part of the century.

"In our version, a grief-stricken woman came to Dr. Buzzard to reverse a curse which had resulted in her sister's death. She explained that she had found a 'conjure jar' under her sister's bed after her death. As she explained this, the actress lifted into the light a Mason jar containing a black chicken's foot and some herbs floating in a reddish liquid. As the actor portraying Dr. Buzzard took the conjure jar from her, the woman fell to her knees and plunged her hands into an oblong box of earth representing the grave. She raised her hands and let the grave dirt flow through the spotlight's beam and onto the stage, shrieking in grief as she did so. The actress's agony was so real that it was easy to forget that this was just a play. It was always a chillingly fun moment in our little production.

"On this particular evening, the last three of us in the

building were preparing to leave when I knelt down by the mock grave to retrieve a prop dropped there. Part of the routine after each show was to smooth out the earth in the box, erasing the deep indentations made by the actress's hands as she dug into it, to make the prop ready for the next performance. But as I put my hands into the dirt to do so, I felt something strange.

"Streams of cool air seemed to be wafting up from the hand prints in the grave. I passed my hands over the rest of the earth but felt nothing. The cool air was coming directly from the marks the hands had made in the dirt, and nowhere else. Thinking that surely it was the result of the Strand's air-conditioning system, I asked one of our group to turn off the AC unit, which they did. Turning off the air conditioner had no effect on the jets of air, which now felt colder than before, rushing out of the hand prints on the mock grave. I asked the others if they felt it. We all did. Then one of the actors stopped dead in their tracks in the audience aisle.

" 'Hey, come feel this. There's a cold spot right here!'

"We rushed over and, sure enough, there was a distinct cold spot in precisely that spot and that spot only. We could all walk through it and tell exactly where it began and where it ended. The air in the building was otherwise deadly still and already getting muggy on this hot night without the AC. Now we were all getting spooked, and not in the fun way either.

"That evening, the performance had been attended by three ghost hunters, or paranormal investigators, from North Carolina. The trio had visited Georgetown many times before and declared it to be a hot spot for ghostly investigation.

"Now, with cold air still pouring up from the on-stage grave and emanating from nowhere in a specific spot in the aisle, we instantly had the same thought. Remembering the line from the movie *Ghostbusters*, someone nervously cracked,

'Who ya gonna call?' We dialed the motel and found the leader of the group, Jayne Ware—sometimes called 'Granny Ghostbuster' in the press—preparing for bed.

" 'You've gotta come back to the theater—something's happening!' we told her in what must have sounded like a symphony of chipmunks on her end of the phone.

" 'I'll be right there,' she said.

"No sooner had we hung up the phone in the Strand's office than things got a lot stranger. On stage, from behind the set, there were whispers—quiet, insistent whispers. We all heard them. And it was clear that they were coming from backstage. We were, of course, the only ones in the building.

"One of our group went out onto the sidewalk to await the arrival of Granny Ghostbuster. I resolved to go backstage. The whispers were not in and of themselves frightening. It sounded like many people talking quietly at once. The only frightening part was that there was no one backstage!

"Our backdrop was simple and inexpensive—wood frames over which were stretched dark blue sheets. The sheets acted as the back wall of the set. As I stepped on stage, my heart was pounding. It was like being on a roller coaster just before the big drop. The whispers were still there as I walked across the stage, put out my hands, and tentatively pushed against the dark blue sheets. I have never been so scared in my life, but I was about to be absolutely terrified. Something on the other side of the sheets pushed back. I withdrew my hands and could hardly speak.

" 'Something is on the other side!' I said weakly.

"I did manage the courage to reach out toward the sheet again, but this time, when I felt the pressure of whatever was on the other side against my palms, I broke into a run across the stage and jumped down, passing the still-present streams of cold air from the grave on my way.

"We had never been more happy to see another living soul than we were when Granny Ghostbuster herself walked in a few moments later. Jayne was calm and very interested in what we had to say. She let us speak our frantic piece, then she walked down the aisle toward the cold spot.

" 'Do you feel it?' we all asked.

"She turned, her face completely peaceful, and nodded.

" 'I feel it. It's here. It's here.'

"We told her about the cold air from the grave, which she confirmed by passing her hands over it, and about the whispering, which had now ceased.

"In the silence, she smiled and said, 'Let's go back up front.'

"In the lobby, Jayne calmed us all down with the air of calm she carried always about with her. She said she wasn't at all surprised at the evening's events.

" 'You're dealing with real people's lives and real people's passions,' she told us. 'All of these old stories, no matter how embellished they may be, are based on a real person's life, and usually on their pain. Dr. Buzzard was real, the conjure you used was real, wasn't it?'

"One of us interrupted, 'It's a rubber chicken's foot that I spray-painted black!'

"Jayne laughed. 'But it *represents* something people felt passionately about. That's what I think the experiences we call ghosts are—representations of the past, impressions or images flash-burnt onto the atmosphere by the strength of the emotion.'

"We had heard this explanation before, but after being scared out of our wits, we wanted a bit more from her.

" 'Why tonight?' asked one of us. 'We do it twice a week. What's so special about tonight?'

"Jayne shrugged. 'A combination of things, probably. A passionate performance. The emotions of the audience. The right temperature. The right amount of humidity in the air.

The perfect combination of all of it. You just got a little closer than you expected to, that's all.'

" 'Will it happen again?' someone asked. 'Because if it does, I quit.'

" 'Probably not like this again, no. But you'll always know they're there.'

"No one dared ask her opinion as to who or what *they* were.

"Jayne concluded, 'Think of it as a compliment, like a standing ovation.'

"And with that, Granny Ghostbuster rose and walked back into the theater, where everything was normal again. No cold spot. No cold air. No whispers. I even had the courage to join the others in walking around the rickety backstage and into the dirt pit where the foundation of the old movie screen had rested. There was, of course, no one there.

"Many years have passed since that night. The show went on for a few more summers past that one. The events of the evening were never repeated. The Strand has a new stage, beneath which rests the dirt pit we used as our dressing room. We in the cast went our separate ways. We grew older. Jayne Ware passed on.

"Sometimes, when passing by the Strand Theatre or attending a performance there, I wonder, did it happen at all? Did our fertile actors' minds, supercharged by the night's performance, create all of it in our heads as a shared delusion? But then that would require one to believe that Granny Ghostbuster had played along.

"If it was real, who were the whisperers? The essence of everyone who had ever been entertained in the old Strand? The essence of the long-ago people we portrayed in our show? And so, before writing this account down, I called on an old friend—one of my fellow cast members.

" 'I've been asked to write about the Strand for a ghost-story book, and I wanted to ask you—'

"His response cut me off sharply and perhaps told me what I needed to know.

"He said, 'I don't want to talk about that night. *Ever.*' "

The ghostly presences have not disappeared over the years.

The Swamp Fox Players have continued to improve the theater. When the lobby and balcony were renovated in 2001, seats for the balcony were brought in from the old Palace Theater. In 2005, a greenroom, dressing rooms, a rehearsal room, and a workshop were added to the rear of the theater.

The presences are still there. When are their sounds most prevalent?

"Mostly, when you are alone in the theater," said Inge Ebert. "There are times when you absolutely have to be alone. Rehearsals are mostly at night. When you get in early and the rest of the people are not there yet, it's like you are disturbing someone. It's like someone is in there. It is not like wood creaking. It's very brief, then it stops, but it gets your attention."

The ghostly presences in the historic Strand Theatre— traces of energy from passionate lives and deaths long ago— may date back many years before the advent of movies. Similar to a film that runs over and over again, the vitality ingrained on the atmosphere here is destined, like history, to repeat itself.